D U

FOLK
TALES

DUBLIN
FOLK
TALES

BRENDAN NOLAN

ILLUSTRATED BY CATHERINE COX

The
History
Press
Ireland

For Rory and Kevin; sons and brothers both.

First published 2012

The History Press Ireland
119 Lower Baggot Street
Dublin 2
Ireland
www.thehistorypress.ie

© Brendan Nolan, 2012
www.dublinfolktales.com
Illustrations © Catherine Cox, 2012

British Library Cataloguing in Publication Data.
A catalogue record for this book is available from the British Library.

ISBN 978 1 84588 728 5

Typesetting and origination by The History Press

CONTENTS

ACKNOWLEDGEMENTS

Thanks to Jack Lynch, master storyteller; Mike Savage; Alan Fitzpatrick; Greg Kenny; David Spain; John Byrne; Jimmy Hickey and Marian Butler, for their help and encouragement; not forgetting my researchers Rita, Rachel, Josh, Holly and Leo.

INTRODUCTION

It is very hard to be a storyteller in Dublin for everyone has a story to tell if you will but listen.

It is not long since Dublin was more of a large town than a city. Most people will know something about the background of any story you choose to tell. Even if they do not know someone in a story, they will know his sister-in-law's friend from down the road, or perhaps their cousin played football against him fourteen years ago come February next. And they lost by one goal in extra time. And they are still blaming the referee for defeat. So, if you are adding colour to a story you must be careful to disguise the characters very well.

Stories are never told the same way twice. The core of the story remains the same but the teller adapts the story for the listener instead of reciting an ancient tale as if it was written in stone, with not a pebble out of place or of a different hue to the original.

Mostly, storytelling is about telling a story well so that both listener and teller create the story together. The role of the storyteller is that of entertainer, historian, philosopher, healer and soothsayer all rolled into one. If you tell a story well, it becomes a real and living tale even if the characters lived thousands of years ago. I have told old stories about real people, only to have someone come to me afterwards to whisper a question asking if I was really talking about Peter, or Paul, or maybe even Mary, when I called the character Dermot. Very few ever identify the real person, and I never, ever confirm anything, for I will tell the story somewhere else to another audience. Next time, I will change it again in some little way.

I tell stories in live settings, to audiences ranging from just two to many hundreds of people, stretching away into the darkness of a theatre, conference hall or festival. I tell stories on radio, online on my website www.brendannolan. ie and in books.

This collection of stories are written, so in that sense, I cannot change them for you when next you read them; but if you happen to re-tell them, you are free to play with the details of the story, so long as you stay true to the core of the tale. For that is the pact between teller and listener: the teller tells true.

In this collection, you have the story of the Pig-woman of Dublin and how she endowed a hospital despite mad rumours about her features, you have the story of the grave robbers stealing bodies for re-sale, the story of the Blood Field linking a battle from a thousand years ago to very real hauntings of today and the story of two Mammies and a Pope about the time the Pope came to Dublin to tell his stories to a million people at a time.

Characters abound in these tales and you will recognise in the older ones the antecedents of today's street chancers and charmers. We hear how two tinkers bested a toll taker on Ha'penny Bridge and how the legless Billy-in-the-Bowl seduced his victims so he could rob and kill them. You will read also of the neighbour of Blessed Matt Talbot, who sold bits of the dead man's bed until there was no more to be had and then produced an unending supply of relics for sale. A seventeenth-century archbishop returns as a ghost after he is publicly hanged and another clergyman is left sitting in the dock for a day after he died because he expired before the judge could sentence him to death. We try to understand how a man could successfully propose marriage to the wrong woman on St Valentine's Day and we wonder just who Molly Malone really was. Wakes and headless coachmen and the quaint customs of honeymooners are all here, including the tragic story of the newlyweds who appeared on the street the following morning to violently attack one another with their new matching hatchets. How a boy negotiated a new pair of shoes after losing one shoe in the river is told here for the first time. Dublin characters Bang Bang, an adult child who shot everyone he met with a large key, and Detective Lugs Brannigan who did his best not to be shot by real crooks with real guns are both here. There is the story of the landlady who actively robbed from her guests while charging them for overnight accommodation and the tale of the television thieves that were unmasked by their dog is told along with the story of the phantom dog of St Patrick's Cathedral. How a married man came to be wearing a green wig while pursuing his girlfriend down Temple Bar is included as is the routing of post office thieves at Christmas by a loaded mother with a gun. The story of Marsh's Library and the runaway teenager is told here, as is the legend of the Holy Coal and the miracle of the woman that walked after years in bed. They say that Little John of Sherwood Forest was hanged in Dublin and we recount that story so you may make up your own mind. You can wonder at the soundness of the verdict in the case that became known as the Ireland's Eye Tragedy and you can wonder at the strange lives of cats in Dead Cat Bounce. Stories from real Dubliners caught up in the Phoenix Park and North Strand bombings are included as is the story of the man that had a few fits too many in the local baker's shop. Another cat appears in the story of Dublin's Hellfire Club, only this time he is the devil. Or, so they say!

You must make up your own mind, for as always, the devil is in the detail of a story well told.

1

THE PIG-WOMAN OF DUBLIN

It is hard to shake a story off when people believe it to be true. They tell others, who tell others, and so on, until the whole world gets to hear it. It happened to one lady in Dublin. No matter what she did or said, it became common belief that, while she was born unblemished in form and from fine stock, she bore the head of a pig.

Dr Steevens' Hospital used to be a major city hospital that catered for the needs of the local population living out along the roads to the west. It was located beside Heuston station and a short distance from Phoenix Park, the Zoological Gardens and the Hibernian Military School. It was a busy place at its height and stories are often told about places where people gather.

It was believed that the mother of its founder had given birth to a baby girl that bore a pig's head. It was also known that the hospital's benefactor was that afflicted child, grown to womanhood and a life of seclusion within the hospital. At least, local folklore said it was so.

Small children heard this story from larger children who heard them from older children and from young adults. And if a parent or grandparent was asked for provenance they would nod and say, 'So I have heard.' Such a generational imprimatur was powerful and resulted in the place being avoided at all costs. Not an easy choice if you faced a medical emergency in the days of rudimentary medical care when surgeons still opened stolen cadavers to learn how the body worked.

Who wanted to say the stories were not true? For who would wish to encounter a human being with a pig's head on a dark Dublin street when weak lamps flickered and shadows danced in between? How would you reason your way out of harm with such a creature? You might run away in daylight, but at night, who was to say what could happen if you stumbled in flight or if the stranger proved to be swifter of foot?

Folk tales and stories travelled from place to place and between the seventeenth and nineteenth centuries a rumour spread across Europe that a number of girls in different places had been born with a normal body but with the head of a swine. That each was of a wealthy family added wonder to the tale. The belief is said to have begun with the story of a pig-faced bride who was offered a choice: to appear to be ugly to her new husband and beautiful to everyone else, or ugly to others and beautiful to her husband. Witchcraft was said to have been involved in the physical appearance of the woman.

She chose to appear best to her husband because he had chosen her while she was afflicted with porcine features, not for her wealth or standing, but for her intrinsic beauty. In time, it being such a heart-warming story, the witchcraft element fell away and the story was presented as triumph over adversity and as good receiving its reward. It was only a short step from a folk tale of witchcraft to a definite narrative about specific individuals.

Typically, the affected child would grow up with some of the characteristics of a pig. She would eat from a trough (which would be made of silver, however, to show there was a difference between her and a real pig) and she would speak with a grunting sound. She would stand to inherit a large fortune, but her parents would be concerned for her wellbeing, following their death. They would try to make arrangements to find a man willing to marry her and to care for her in their stead or they would use their fortune to endow a hospital on condition that the hospital take care of her for the remainder of her unmarried life.

In Dublin, this story settled on the unwilling person of the philanthropist Griselda Steevens who lived in the second half of the seventeenth century and the first half of the eighteenth century. Her twin brother Richard was a doctor who pre-deceased Griselda by some thirty years. The family was wealthy with an income assured from various non-medical interests. Richard's will stipulated that on the death of his twin, the family income was to be used to provide a hospital for the poor of Dublin.

Although Dr Steevens' will stated that work on the hospital would not begin until Griselda's death, she ordered that work commence before her death in 1720, keeping back only sufficient funds for her own keeping. Her sole condition was that she would be granted apartments in the hospital in which to live out her days.

Despite being a philanthropist and almsgiver to the poor and needy, Griselda became the focus of the pig-woman story. A gargoyle above the entrance of the hospital was offered as material proof of the story. It peered down, it was solemnly stated, not to protect the hospital from malevolent fortune, but to remind all that refusing alms to a street person was not wise if you wanted your own family to remain healthy.

Griselda's mother was said to have answered the door to a beggar woman while pregnant with the twins. According to Dublin lore, which closely matched the European stories, the pregnant mother told the beggar woman who was seeking help for her children to go away from her door. More specifically, she was reported to have said the woman should take away her litter of pigs from her door. This shocking demand was rewarded with a curse, placed on her by the poor woman, that the child in her womb would be born a pig. The result was that Griselda was born with the face and head of a pig, as a punishment to her mother. Somehow or another, the second child in her womb escaped this curse.

In fact, Griselda did indeed have a medical condition which manifested itself as she grew older. She was said to have had suffered from a disorder of the eyes, that caused her to wear a veil while in daylight to protect her eyes from strong light. She wore the veil even when passing through the gardens of the hospital she had funded. Her sartorial style reinforced the belief that she was so ugly she could not bear that anyone might gaze upon her.

The unfortunate Griselda, aware of such reports, began sitting on an open balcony to allow passers-by to see her perfectly normal face, albeit with a distressing condition of the eyes to contend with. Failing to counter the persistent story, Griselda commissioned a portrait of herself in her finery and had it hung in the main hall of the hospital to show she was a perfectly normal being, complete in all relevant parts. Even so, most people preferred a portrait hanging in a neighbouring pub which showed Griselda with a pig's head. That there were similar portraits of pig-women hanging in other European cities made no difference to the Dublin story. Griselda passed away on 18 March 1746, at the fine age of ninety-three but the story of her supposed affliction remains on the streets of Dublin to this day.

In 1865, more than a hundred years later, the story was strong enough for Sheridan Le Fanu to use it in his novel *Uncle Silas*, the story of Maud Ruthyn, a wealthy heiress who

lives in a secluded house. Numerous men desire to marry her
to secure her money. Nothing unusual in that for a novel
device, but the book includes a Bretagne ballad, believed to
be the work of Le Fanu himself, about a pig-faced woman,
told to Maud by her governess Madame de la Rougierre.

This lady was neither pig nor maid,
And so she was not of human mould;
Not of the living nor the dead.
Her left hand and foot were warm to touch;
Her right as cold as a corpse's flesh!
And she would sing like a funeral bell, with a ding-dong
tune.
The pigs were afraid, and viewed her aloof;
And women feared her and stood afar.
She could do without sleep for a year and a day;
She could sleep like a corpse, for a month and more.
No one knew how this lady fed—
On acorns or on flesh.
Some say that she's one of the swine-possessed,
That swam over the sea of Gennesaret.
A mongrel body and demon soul.
Some say she's the wife of the Wandering Jew,
And broke the law for the sake of pork;
And a swinish face for a token doth bear,
That her shame is now, and her punishment coming.

Le Fanu spent the first eleven years of his life, from
about 1815, living in the Hibernian Military School in
the nearby Phoenix Park where his father was a minister of religion. The family and their son would certainly
have known of the story of Griselda Steevens. Le Fanu
published the *Evening Mail*, much read by the moneyed
classes of Dublin. He was one of the earliest writers of
Irish Gothic horror stories and recognised an intriguing
story when he heard one.

Le Fanu was not alone in perpetuating the legend of the pig-faced woman of Dublin. Medical students at Dr Steevens' Hospital in the early nineteenth century were shown a silver feeding trough, alleged to have belonged to Griselda Steevens. Even if they were displayed as students' high jinks and pranks, it shows that belief in the story persisted in the institution formed by a philanthropist who went to a great deal of effort to prove the story of her appearance to be a false one.

Debunkers of the folk tale say there is no contemporary evidence to suggest that story was prevalent during Griselda's lifetime: yet a folk tale endures into modern times that there lived a pig-woman in Dr Steeven's hospital and it was Griselda. For a good story is a good story, true or no.

2

SACK-'EM-UPS

It's hard to imagine that when you die someone may want to come along and steal your body so that surgeons in a hospital can cut you open to see how a human body functions. Such was the case in Dublin up to the nineteenth century, when medical schools were in constant need of bodies for both students and medical staff to study. Dubliners called the body-snatchers Sack-'em-Ups.

The 1752 Murder Act stipulated that only corpses of executed murderers could be used for dissection. However, the thirst for knowledge meant that the supply of bodies of hanged criminals could not meet the demand. Before the invention of refrigeration, bodies decayed very quickly and became unsuitable for study. As a result, the medical profession turned to body-snatchers to supply corpses fresh enough to be examined. Such was the demand across the two islands that Dublin bodies were often exported to Britain, as swiftly as possible.

The offence was treated only as a misdemeanour and the penalty for being caught was not onerous. High return at low risk meant that many people took up the trade of grave robber across Britain and Ireland. Such was the case until the Anatomy Act of 1832 changed the gravity of the crime while also leading to a wider selection of potential sources. The act gave physicians, surgeons and students legal access to corpses that were unclaimed after death, in particular those who died in prison or the workhouse. But the practice of grave robbing continued in Dublin, for some time.

In 1842, five watch towers were erected in Glasnevin cemetery and bloodhounds were used to patrol the cemetery at night to deter the theft of newly buried bodies. On the other side of the city, Malachi Horan, the storyteller, related an account of how a mother's body was stolen on her first night in the ground, in Saggart. Her adult son was so upset at what he saw as his failure to guard her body that he neither ate, drank nor slept for three days or nights, after which he expired himself. His neighbours were so angry at the needless suffering of the son and the theft of his mother's body that they mounted an armed guard on his grave through the nights that followed. It was the practice of the Sack-'em-Ups to pay local informants for news of fresh internments. No doubt, they soon heard of their pending good fortune in extracting two bodies from one grave.

The watchers' patience and diligence were rewarded when the Sack-'em-Ups began to dig in darkness in the silent Saggart graveyard. The watching men, once they were sure of their target, fired a volley into the shadowy Sack-'em-Ups. One was shot dead and fell among the graves.

He was discovered to be a medical student and son of the famous Surgeon Colles of Dr Steevens' Hospital. Colles was a professor of anatomy, surgery and physiology, but whether he was aware of the activities of his student son, we do not know. In a strange twist to the story, Colles is said to have been the only man knowledgeable enough to save the boxer Dan Donnelly's arm from amputation following injuries sustained in a street fight with some sailors when Donnelly protected a woman they were attacking in a side street. Donnelly, in turn, was to be a victim of the Sack-'em-Ups himself when he died and was interred.

To this day, Dr Steevens' hospital is known to Dubliners as the 'Butchers' Hospital'. It's an appellation that is not so much a comment on the quality of its medical care as an old description of its staff and their practices. The hospital lies not far from the Bully's Acre at Kilmainham. The site was a communal burial ground and was easily accessed.

Heinous as their crimes were, grave robbers or Sack-'em-Ups were not murderers, though they dealt in death. Some people called them Resurrectionists because they hauled out the bodies from the grave and re-integrated them into society; even if the dead person's participation was not as active as it been prior to their demise.

There was no financial charge levied to be buried in Bully's Acre. Many of the city's poor were buried there, though no one seems to know how many bodies were interred there for few records were kept but there were many and they were the poorest of the people. During the cholera epidemic of 1832, thousands of people's remains were buried, as expeditiously as possible, in Bully's Acre. The burial ground at Kilmainham was a prime target of the Sack-'em-Ups. They would come with wooden shovels, ropes and hooks to haul the recently dead from the ground, out to the road, and onto a horse and cart for taking away to a no-questions-asked medical client. Their horses were shod with leather to quieten their step in the dead of night. For if the crime was a misdemeanour in the eyes of the law it was a scurrilous act to the bereaved who would act decisively against any grave robbers they could find.

In Irish winters a heavy cotamore coat that reached the ankles was worn by those that worked outdoors. Attached to it was a cape and beneath the coat were corduroy or moleskin breeches above grey stockings. The Sack-'em-Ups were dressed thus when they entered the burial grounds in search of new cadavers; their very appearance creating fear in any beholders foolish enough to be out in the darkness of a graveyard when body-snatchers were on the move.

Mostly they worked on information supplied by informants; but if the thieves failed to find a suitable body they could take away teeth from the dead, as an alternative reward for effort. A set of good teeth could command a pound at a time when there were four farthings to a penny and 240 pennies to a pound. Many items that the poor purchased were priced at a farthing, so a set of teeth could be a valuable item, whatever about their new owner being aware of their provenance.

To retrieve entire bodies, the Sack-'em-Ups dug at the head of a fresh grave to get at the new body. They quietened their handiwork by using a wooden spade that made less noise than its metal equivalent if any loose stones were struck. The removed soil was stacked on body-size sacks laid out on the ground in as neat a manner as darkness and weather conditions allowed.

When they reached the coffin, the thieves broke open part of the casket to expose the upper body and head of the dead person. A small person slithered down to put a rope or hook around the neck of the corpse and it was unceremoniously dragged out into the world once more. Once the body was secured above ground, the soil was tipped back into the excavation. The site was made to look as undisturbed as was possible so that the theft might not be discovered for as long as possible.

However, public and private resentment came to a head when the body of boxer Dan Donnelly was stolen from Bully's Acre. Crowds took to the streets in anger when the news spread. Donnelly was a native of Townsend Street in the docks area of Dublin. Born in 1788, he was the ninth child of seventeen, in a time when families were large and times were hard. Dan worked as a wandering carpenter early in his adult life. But it was as a bare-knuckle boxer that he achieved fame and a degree of fortune before his death at the age of thirty-two years, in February 1820.

Boxing bouts had no time limits at the time, so that two men fought to exhaustion or victory before cheering onlookers. Donnelly's most famous victory was against George Cooper, the heavy-weight champion of Britain, whom he beat on the Curragh of Kildare. But fame is fleeting. It is said that drinking copious amounts of cold water after a later fight killed Donnelly in the end. By then, he had failed as a pub owner several times and was broke once more.

Thousands of people turned out for his funeral and internment at Bully's Acre. The cemetery was claimed, rightly or wrongly, to contain the grave of Brian Boru, the High King of Ireland. Donnelly was no sooner buried than his body was stolen by the Sack-'em-Ups and sold to a Dublin surgeon named Hall. But Hall was not to be in possession of the body of the people's champion for long.

It was soon established which surgeon had paid cash on delivery for the body of Dan Donnelly, the people's champion. Tense discussions took place between Donnelly's followers and Hall over the body. Accepting that the remains must be returned, Hall negotiated the removal of the right arm from the body and the attached shoulder blade in order to study the muscle structure. When this was agreed, the body was re-buried in the Kilmainham graveyard with due reverence, where it lay undisturbed from then on.

Donnelly's right arm was to do more travelling than the rest of his body ever did. It was displayed in a pub for many years in the town of Kilcullen, County Kildare, not far from the scene of its most famous fight. After that, it travelled the world to appear in various exhibitions of Irish interest.

The cemetery, where its companion arm and the rest of Donnelly's body fell into decay is no longer in use and there are no Sack-'em-Ups in operation any more.

Another story told about the robbers relates how a Peter Harkan, a well-known Dublin surgeon and teacher of anatomy, died in Bully's Acre in the early 1800s while on

a corpse-stealing exhibition. He was spotted in the cemetery by a party of watchmen who chased him and his assistants. The assistants crossed the perimeter wall in time but Harkan was caught by the legs by the watchmen. Harkan's pupils pulled his upper body to free him but such was the counter force used by both parties that the grave robber Harkan died in the graveyard that he had come to rob.

Some say it was a fitting end for him, others argue that Harkan and the resurrectionists performed a public duty in expanding the knowledge of the human body. It would have been nice, however, if they had asked permission of the bereaved before digging people's bodies up again and spiriting them into the Dublin night while they were freshly dead and not yet at their eternal rest.

When you die that should be the end of it. Otherwise, what's the point of death?

3

BLOOD FIELD

Ghost stories were told aplenty in olden times in Ireland. They were told with such conviction that people believed them. Many things that seem in darkness to be real, may in daylight seem more a fancy of the night. Nonetheless, people paid attention when the storyteller told the tale, for who knew what might befall them on the dark roads when night fell?

Reports of ghostly appearances and hauntings died away when rural Ireland was electrified in the twentieth century under a scheme that brought connection to the national grid for most houses, however remote and inaccessible. Dancing candle and shadows thrown by paraffin lamp gave way to a steadier light.

The wandering spirits also began to disappear to the detriment of ghostly storytelling, but to the greater peace of local inhabitants. Reports of strange shapes and appearances in darkened rooms fell away. However, a working clairvoyant relates a twenty-first-century story concerning a house in County Dublin in which Michael, a six-year-old boy, lived with his parents and family.

A frightened Michael told his parents that he was seeing visions at night of soldiers from an army of long ago, moving towards and away from a battle. They were passing along the road outside their home. Some of the warriors had even passed through their semi-detached home, he said. His parents rationalised the stories as the imaginings of a child. While not entirely dismissing the boy's stories, they were content when he went asleep each night, for his dreams were waking dreams and all the more unsettling for that. While he slept, silence settled on the upper floors of the small home on a modern estate in the suburb of Clondalkin in the west of the city.

However, the clairvoyant was called in by Michael's father when he, the father, encountered an armed soldier on the stairs of the house, giving credence to the boy's story and frightening the adult man as much as it terrified the child. The soldier passed by without a word and seemed to pass out of the building without touching the closed, locked and secured door. The father then fervently agreed with his son that there was indeed something stirring in their home.

The clairvoyant came to the house and did what she could for the dark curly-haired boy and his family so that calm could be returned. She sat with the boy and talked about what they could both see. She helped him draw in his special dreams until they were finally closed off to the boy's vision.

Before the window closed down, the clairvoyant gazed at the visions with Michael and through him they saw an encampment of a time from long ago, on the streets and roads where the new houses now stood. There were tents and weapons stacked together and defences raised around the encampment against sudden attack by the opposing army.

In the distance, at night, there were red and yellow bonfires blazing in the sky. Flickering shadows of men passed before and behind the fire. At other times, women could be seen on a battlefield seeking fallen family members and administering to the wounded and the dying. Armed soldiers with long, matted hair tucked into their belts, clad in makeshift body armour and armed with shields and swords and long two-handed battle-axes passed by the boy's home in the middle of a housing estate, without a word.

A man clad in sackcloth lingered nearby, on another day, waiting for someone to come by, amidst the crying of grown men and the rolling sounds of mortal conflict from a battle-field not far away. Bodies of the shocked dead and terrified wounded were piled high and moved back on creaking two-wheeled carts, drawn by weary oxen away from the battle. The dead were tumbled to one side where they lay; the wounded were tended with rudimentary care and dressings. Some of these returned to battle, some withered and passed away in their own time.

There was nothing the watchers could do except gaze at the drama unfolding before them. In time, the images dimmed and vanished from the ken of the little family. When all was quiet once more, the clairvoyant moved on.

At the same time in another house in the same area, a young mother had an unexpected guest each night when she told bedtime stories to her two young children. A small boy came down the stairs from an attic room and sat upon the steps staring through the banisters until the stories were told once more. He was dressed in clothes of another time. He never spoke, but walked quietly to the top of the house when the story ended. When the adults went to search for him, he was nowhere to be found, no matter how hard they looked. Yet each night there he was again waiting for a story to be told.

In time, he stopped appearing.

In the same area, many years earlier, Aisling, now a grown woman, lived as a young girl, before acres of modern houses were planted in the verdant fields. She had wandered free across rolling meadows in the summer of her childhood. That is, except for one field which she avoided, for the strong smell that came from it repulsed her senses when she approached the enclosure. Though she was too young to recognise the smell's origin as blood, in her childish way Aisling called it the 'Weirdie Field'. She saw with young eyes that the grass was a deeper green and lusher than the surrounding fields. She felt there was a restless silence about the place and she did not like it. Aisling continued to play in the other fields and didn't let the 'Weirdie Field' bother her.

As an adult, living elsewhere in Dublin, and with the fields of her childhood now covered in housing estate after housing estate, with housing stock rolling across hill and plain alike, and the city approaching ever closer, she researched the lore of her home place to satisfy an adult curiosity. She discovered the name of the field to be the 'Blood Field', in the old tongue. It was named so in a time when names were descriptions of places and the events that occurred there. It was where a battle had taken place, more than a thousand years ago, and where it seemed ghosts of the fallen lingered on awaiting some resolution.

A Viking settlement once stood many fields away from Aisling's childhood home, she discovered. It was ruled over by Olaf the White, a Viking chieftain who was named King of Dublin by the Vikings. The settlement was in the townland of Dunawley (Olaf's Fort) in the general area of Clondalkin. Not content with Irish tribute and subjugation, Olaf and his men sailed down the nearby Liffey in their warships and across the Irish Sea in a great fleet of fighting men to raid in Northumbria, in or around AD 850. While he was away, Gaithine, an Irish chieftain, raided the Viking settlement to wrest control from the Viking garrison. Much blood was shed in the battle for supremacy between the opposing forces.

It was to be a further sixteen years before Olaf returned to Dublin, laden with booty from his warring escapades. He and his belligerent warriors came with great determination to tackle the Irish fighters. Further killing and mayhem ensued across the open fields in the highlands above the valley of the River Liffey, before the warring was done. Thousands of souls perished through those years of attrition and retribution. We know not what matters may lie unfinished among the souls of the dead.

One-on-one combats were fought to finality in the midst of huge battles where thousands of desperate men killed their foes. When it was over, the bodies of the fallen were covered over where they lay. The soil was enriched by their spilt blood and their crushed bones. In time, rotting carcasses produced bone meal that fertilised the blood field where green grass grew high above where they lay, forever stilled.

Aisling moved away to her new married home. Her childhood home is no more; it was sacrificed for a new road from Dublin to the west, many years ago now. Michael's modern house has been set to rest; no more visions intrude on his life. His father has seen nothing since the clairvoyant left and his mother does not speak about it at all. But there is a sense of unfinished business in the air. A sense of watchers watching. For what we know not.

In modern times, a local businessman met an associate in an overspill shopping-centre car park, to hand over some documents relating to some business they had together. On a warm July day in West Dublin they shook hands and parted. But as the businessman turned to step back into his car, a breeze ran across the otherwise empty car park and he shivered. Someone had stepped on his grave.

He looked across to where some very old trees grew in the distance. He fancied he saw some flitting dark shadows moving beneath the trees, but when he blinked and looked again, he could see nothing. All was still. Heat returned to his head and he turned back to his car to leave as expeditiously as possible. That car park is built close to the old Blood Field. It was daylight. Shadows of firelight were not at play. That businessman said he will not return there.

Unless he must ... For who knows what lies beneath or beside the Blood Field of Dublin? Some matter lies unfinished there. There are some shadows that not even the brightest of lights can dispel and some stories of which we know nothing.

4

Two Mammies
and a Pope

It's a traumatic time for anyone when a mother is lost. Tom lost his mother among a million people in Phoenix Park, and his mother-in-law somewhere on a Dublin beach in high summer.

Tom's mother-in-law had invited all her adult children and their lovers and spouses to go to Portmarnock Beach on a sunny Sunday afternoon. However, she caught a bus to Dollymount Strand instead, because she had been to Portmarnock too many times before. Her family spent the day walking the sands looking for her. They tramped in and out of the dunes, had rows, said they were sorry, had a quick hug in this time of need, and walked on again. They stared out to sea with their hands to their eyes in case she had been kidnapped by pirates or had swum out to a shipwreck and found a new life there with survivors on Ireland's Eye beside Dublin Bay.

When they returned home, she was sitting in her favourite armchair eating toast and drinking sweet tea with her feet in a basin of cold water, as if there hadn't been enough water in the sea at Dollymount to satisfy her needs. It was the first intimation her family had that she was abandoning them and her howling grandchildren for a quieter life of her own. She said Dollymount was grand if you managed not to be run over by learner drivers practising their driving, while you were having a doze in the sun. When Tom asked her why she sitting in a basin of water, she said she thought her feet were a little sunburnt from the beach, so the water was an after-sun measure that cost nothing to prepare.

Tom's own mother had abandoned her children in a different way. She went off to see a man in Phoenix Park one fine Saturday in September. At least her children and grandchildren knew she was somewhere among a million other people on the Fifteen Acres gathered to see Pope John Paul II appear on top of a grassy mound. Tom's family home was beside the park and he and his siblings and pals all flocked to their home on the night before the Pope's appearance in Phoenix Park. They slept all over the place. There were bodies everywhere in the house that night, and their mother lied and said that she was delighted to see them all back home once more. 'It's lovely,' she said as she went off early to bed.

Excitable small children will wake early in the morning, especially if they are in a strange house. Well, the assembled clan's youngest kids did so, with much recrimination from their sleep-deprived parents. When they woke they found their granny had run away from home. She had made secret arrangements with old neighbours that they would all go to see the Pope together and off she went before the house was astir. Not a chick nor a child saw her go. She was like a thief in the night. Only she stole away her offspring's certainties.

Everyone was worried about her and went to the park to look for her. The Pope started to tell everyone how happy he was to be there and everyone cheered and clapped and said, 'Isn't it a grand day,' and 'Not a drop of rain to be seen anywhere.' No sight of the errant woman could be found. They all headed home, worn out, but feeling pious, hoping that that extra prayer they said would make the missing woman show up, safe and sound.

On their return, they found a queue of people sneaking into their home from the footpath outside. Their mother,

now home safe and well and full of sisterly love, was providing restroom facilities, in the Name of God, to anyone
taken short and willing to queue. It was a work of mercy she
said, God's work, providing a warm toilet sea and a flush-
able cistern as divine intervention on a day when a million
people were on the move around the park. There was no
use arguing. Her children and her children's children soon
found themselves pressed into service as loo-queue admin-
istrators while the mammy graciously accepted the plaudits
of a relieved populace. Some say to this day that it was her
finest hour.

Tom's mother-in-law, the beach lover, in departing for
the park from a different parish, managed to do so without
encumbrance of any kind either. Though she had a large
family, she behaved as a single woman on the way to see
a holy man from Poland on his first visit to her town of
Dublin. She went, she saw, she heard, she returned and
had toast and tea and a dip in a basin of cold water in
her house while she watched
highlights of the visit on
television, in colour.

While in the park,
she even waved at the
handsome man on the
back of the converted lorry
as he was driven
around the park
to wave hello to
the faithful col-
lected who had
not been able to
get close enough to
see him on his raised
altar. More than
a million people
had brought fold-

ing picnic chairs with them into the park and were corralled into temporary enclosures of 1,000 souls each. The enclosures were surrounded by sturdy blue nylon rope. The Popemobile, built on the back of a Ford D model truck, travelled up and down wide aisles between the corrals while everyone fell into ecstasy at the good of it all. Everyone was taken up in the euphoria of that September Saturday in Phoenix Park, when the Polish Pope blessed all and sundry whether they wanted a blessing or not.

In time, when the afterglow of that momentous occasion had faded away, a strange thing happened. Both women, Tom's mother and Tom's mother-in-law went on a package holiday to see how they might get on. They enjoyed themselves so much they went together once a year for years afterwards, and rigorously ignored one another for the rest of the year. Their *modus operandi* was to meet on a given date once a year, in Bewley's Oriental Café on Westmoreland Street, and to read the brochures and advertisements together, before going along to a travel agent to pay a deposit on the holiday. For both women, this was a sacred day to be approached with due reverence. They cleared their diaries well in advance, went early to bed the night before, rose early the next morning, went to mass, and then caught a free bus into town from their respective addresses.

So this year they found themselves in Italy, near Castel Gondolfo where the Pope goes on his holidays. The two Dublin mammies decided this was a sign from heaven. It would only be polite to call in and say hello and to bring the decent man up to speed on what had happened in Dublin since his visit there. However, when they tried to have a reunion with him, they were run off by the guards at the gate, who said they were fed up with Dubliners turning up looking to share their picnic sandwiches with his Holiness.

So, Tom's mother-in-law borrowed a bottle of holy water from Tom's mother and emptied it discreetly in a corner of the Pope's palace grounds. They wrote a message for the

Pope and put it in the holy water bottle and threw it over the wall. They waited a while to see if anyone would throw the bottle back over, and when no one did, they went home. When Tom went to pick up the two mammies at the airport he could only wonder and what they had got up to while they were away from their native island.

There was one thing certain, until the days they both left this world, neither of them ever asked any of their family to go on holiday with them. They did, however, leave word that the Pope might be writing to them soon, when he had a minute to spare. But whatever way the bottle landed it must have become lost in the weeds in the garden, for their families are still waiting for a postcard from the Pope to say how he got on on his holidays. Though it is unlikely to come since he has since passed away. Some say he will be made a saint before very much longer and there is a man that lives near Phoenix Park who says prayers every night and morning that it might be so.

Do you remember the miles and miles of blue nylon rope that was used to make corrals in the park on the big day? Well, the local handyman who goes by the name of Jack Ladd gathered up enough of it to lay out a full marathon course if he was ever contracted to do so. This rope he coiled around and around itself until it resembled a great sea monster come to rest in the valley of the Liffey. When asked if he was being dishonest in doing this or, indeed, if it was outright theft of the Pope's property, he replied that he was simply minding it for him lest it be stolen. The Holy Father only needed to call to Jack's house and he could have as much of the rope, or all of it, back on demand. Until then, he would mind it for him with due reverence.

But since that Pope was now on the assembly line to sainthood, Jack made no secret of the fact that he was planning on selling the rope, a mounted inch at a time, to those seeking a religious relic of the new saint. In the meantime, he uses bits of it to tie up anything that needs tying up on a job around the town. Boats of local fishermen belonging to the angler's club are all tied up now with bits of the Pope's rope. Whether people believe in the power of a Pope's blessing or not, it is an undisputable fact that not one single boat has foundered on the river since the Pope came to town. It's the sort of thing that the two mammies knew all the time. It was what they were trying to tell him when they threw the bottle over the wall. 'All is well in Dublin,' said the note in fair handwriting. But a soon to be canonised Pope knew that all along.

5

THE HA'PENNY BRIDGE

The River Liffey has had many bridges thrown over it. Most of them carry both people and wheeled traffic, but a few are for pedestrians only.

With an abundance of bridges now available, we do not think about how we would cross the river if the bridges weren't there, these days. Earlier citizens and visitors crossed over the river using fords when the tidal river was at low tide. Then walls were built to lessen flooding as port commerce demanded a hard standing be provided at the water's edge. The odd bridge was built to convey materials to the other side. Here and there, ferries took people from one side to the other and there was a commercial charge for doing so. A number of ferries operated from the Temple Bar area on the southern side of Liffey Street and on the other.

Crow Street Theatre, the chief theatre in the city, lay on the southern side of the city. Many people crossed over to attend its productions. Then a proposal was made to replace seven ferries with a single-span metal bridge at the Bagino Slip. It would exact a toll for its use in crossing over.

An Alderman Beresford and William Walsh joined together to erect the bridge as a commercial enterprise. It opened for business in 1816 and was formally named Wellington Bridge, but was known to most Dubliners as the Metal Bridge, at least in its early days. Arthur Wellesley,

1st Duke of Wellington, had just defeated Napoleon Bonaparte at the Battle of Waterloo, so it seemed appropriate to call the bridge after him. Wellesley was born in a fine house on Merrion Street and was the only Dubliner to be elected Prime Minister of the United Kingdom.

The bridge was the only pedestrian bridge on the Liffey until the Millennium Bridge was opened upstream in 2000. It was cast at Coalbrookdale in Shropshire in England. The right to exact tolls was set for a period of one hundred years from 1816. Paying tolls to cross the relatively short span was subject to some resentment among the populace and any way that could be used to circumvent the toll was to be applauded by the common man.

The adjacent Bachelors Walk and Ormond Quay were populated for many years by the city's auction rooms. People brought their household goods, including beds and wardrobes to be sold at auction there. Those that wanted these second-hand goods came to bid for them. It made this a very busy area of the city, with milling masses of people either collecting or depositing all kinds of merchandise into and out of a myriad of premises along the quays. In the evening, theatre goers crossed the bridge along with ordinary folk going about their daily lives as best they could.

The story of the pair of tinkers who took exception to paying the toll in pursuit of their trade is a battle of wits and triumph, and is not unlike the history of a wonderful night on the town. Some claim to recollect all the little events which lead up to the climax of the story, but few can recollect their order or the exact time they occurred, which makes all the difference to their value or importance.

The toll had been set at a half penny, of which there were some 480 in an Irish pound of the day. But it was still more than the tinkers would pay. After a while, the crossing came to be known as the Ha'penny Bridge, as well as its official name of Wellington Bridge and its unofficial moniker of the

Metal Bridge. To confuse matters even further, the present-day official name for the bridge is the Liffey Bridge.

In its original form, the bridge had a space at either end where a person stepped through a turnstile to pay the toll and then proceeded across the bridge. In those very early days, a toll taker collected the ha'pennies of crossing pedestrians of all classes and creeds. It was thus when the pair of travelling tinkers arrived at the crossing. The tinkers, or workers in tin and travelling menders of metal household utensils, repaired and replaced objects made of tin on the spot, usually at the person's residence or place of business.

They were just some of the many artisans to be found on the streets of Dublin at this time. Bread firms employed men who drove two-wheeled horse carts to deliver freshly baked breads and confectionary to the shops and houses in the city. Laundrymen, wearing uniforms and caps, delivered and collected laundry in the days before the domestic washing machine replaced such activities. Coal men carted coal for the city's coal merchants on four-wheeled lorries. The tolling of the bell on an independent bellman's lorry showed he had coal for sale; when it was silenced he was finished selling for now. Vegetable sellers and fishwives passed by, on their way from the city markets. Newspaper sellers called out the headlines of the day to attract buyers to the paper. In the midst of this hubbub, our pair of tinkers, Johnny and Paudge, approached the toll taker in their most civil manner.

The busy keeper heard the murmur of two voices, where only shortly before he had been listening to the sleepy, hissing, grating sound of a scissors-grinder's wheel as the sturdy Paudge sharpened up knives for Molly, a passing fishwife who had a nice smile and dancing eyes and curled hair worn to her shoulder to show she was not spoken for yet. Charming as she was, Paudge made sure she paid over the few coins agreed for the work, before she walked off pushing her cart with the day's offerings laid out for sale for the crowds to examine.

Where Paudge had been working, he was now standing beside Johnny who was the spokesperson for the pair of them. Johnny was a taller figure than his partner. He wore a dilapidated chimney hat on his head which stood out among the flat caps of the working Dubliners who were passing by. He touched his hat respectfully as he approached the toll man. He asked how much the price of crossing the bridge might be for a working man that did not earn very much at all, and who had earned even less this week past. The keeper said it was a half penny, as everyone that had any business on the bridge well knew. He looked past Johnny to where Paudge stood with most of their paraphernalia strewn about his person. They travelled light for their work was itinerant and they had no use for heavy tools and had no horse or pack animal to carry it for them.

Paudge tipped his own hat at the keeper to show he was part of the transaction, but he was content to allow the others to discuss the matter between them, as men of commerce might. Johnny asked if there was an allowance for someone crossing on foot. 'It's a pedestrian bridge,' the busy keeper snapped back at him, all the while watching that nobody slipped past without paying their fair share. Was there any discount if two people crossed over at the same time and did not return? It was well known that tinkers could not keep still, and it would be unusual for one to return over a bridge once he had gone to the bother of crossing over to the other side, in the first place. To make the proposition more attractive, Johnny told the keeper that some day they would be back again and would most certainly use the bridge once more and would pay the toll all over again on that occasion. 'The toll is a ha'penny,' the keeper replied sternly, to show that he would speak civilly to anyone for a time, but beyond that, he was a busy man.

Johnny stepped away after giving thanks to the man for his forthright answers. He and Paudge then wandered away a little from the bridge to appear as if they were no

longer interested in crossing over. In fact, they did so only
to regroup and review the situation now that the reconnoi-
tre had been completed. There were other ways of crossing
the Liffey. Other bridges did not require any payment at all,
but the challenge was there now and Paudge and Johnny
were determined to cross over the Metal Bridge. They were
equally determined they were not going to hand over the
full amount demanded. For if they were not natives of the
city, they were natives of the country and deserved to be
accommodated in their travels as much as any local person
might be.

They waited until the flow of people had risen up once
more and the keeper was busier than he had been all morning. Paudge stepped forward and asked a question of the toll
taker. 'Do you charge anything, Sir, for luggage, or for what
a man may carry over on his back?' he asked. The keeper
looked at the well-built man in front of him. Paudge was
festooned with all the tools of his trade, and held the sharp-
ening wheel in a maw of a hand. The wheel looked like the
plaything of a privileged child in a nursery in one of the big
houses of Dublin. The keeper responded saying that there
was no extra charge for luggage over
and above the half-penny toll, but that
it must be paid. 'Thank you Sir',
said Paudge and he stepped back
a little to hunch down. To the
toll taker's astonishment
he saw Johnny come
running along the path
to leap up on the back
of the crouching man.
Paudge straightened
up. His thick arms held
Johnny's skinny legs as
safely as if they were
bolted together. His

hands held their tools and equipment, Johnny's hands held the rest and away they went for the toll bridge like that.

When the toll taker tried to stop them, Paudge reminded him that he had said there was no charge for luggage and poor Johnny, having taken faint, was now his burden to carry across the bridge. As he moved on Johnny dropped the single ha'penny piece into the hand of the astonished toll taker. 'God bless you Sir,' said a contented Johnny as the pair crossed the bridge. 'We'll see you the next time we are in Dublin. It surely is a fine bridge you have, God bless it and all who cross over it.' And with that they were gone.

6

BILLY~IN~THE~BOWL

Nowadays, Dublin City sprawls out into the surrounding counties, but these areas were once fields, farms and small villages, where the inhabitants lived a rustic life, within sight of the city. You would not have suspected that a killer once waited for his victims in the quietness of the leafy lanes that led into the city.

There was great interaction between the urban and rural lifestyles, with many of the farm and big-house workers of County Meath and Dublin travelling back and forth to the city on business both social and personal. Life had a slower pace in eighteenth-century Dublin, with public transport very much a thing of the future; people walked, rode on horses, or travelled on carts and coaches drawn by horses, donkeys, or asses. The houses they passed were not new dwellings; they were dwellings of an older stock, some well maintained and some with weathered and peeling fascias in need of attention and repair. Their sagging slate roofs sported tufts of errant green grass hanging over and from rain gullies. Moss spread across old thatch as it willed. Shop floors, in the many small premises along the way, were sprinkled with sawdust, to absorb the muck of a journey.

A journey experienced many times can tire the imagination. Anything that entertains or excites the traveller on the road is to be welcomed. If there is a storyteller, a singer or

someone who would play a tune or two along the way they
are greeted warmly and listened to. This attraction to diversion was a flaw that some vagabonds used to their advantage.
One such character in the north city used a birth defect to
his advantage, in enticing maid servants to halt and to listen
to him.

Billy-in-the-Bowl was an unusual man in that he had
been born without legs. Since everyone finds their own way
of moving about, he developed great strength in his upper
body to help him travel around in a large bowl fortified
with iron. He was to be seen in the Oxmantown neighbourhood, where, with his personality and his soft demeanour,
he charmed maid servants, in particular, coming in from
County Meath to the city. Billy-in-the-Bowl found that
hanging about the quiet streets of Stoneybatter and the
green lanes of adjoining Grangegorman served his purpose
best. We do not know Billy's surname, but we do know that
once Billy gained notoriety, many who came after him with
a mobility impediment and who used similar ways of getting
about were granted the same nickname. Billy-in-the-Bowl
became a brand name almost. Though not all these Billys
ended their days in ignominy.

As he developed into manhood, Billy made himself available for the amusement of the simple servant maids as they
passed by. His good humour and charm were welcomed by
the women along the quiet lanes; he was well liked and
considered to be harmless enough. So much so, that whenever he called at the back door of a big house seeking a little
help, his bowl was filled with beef, with bread, or whatever
there was plenty of in the household. The fact that he was
already acquainted with most of the young female staff did
him no harm.

It was said that nature compensated for his curtailment
of movement by giving him fine dark eyes, an aquiline nose,
a well-formed mouth, dark curling locks, and a body and
arms of Herculean power. His disability, coupled with his

handsome features, touched the hearts of those susceptible to pity and compassion. Many a young woman fell in love with the handsome man so tragically constricted by nature. 'Would that it were different,' more than one sighed. 'It was criminal,' others said.

Those with a more sober view of life, however, dismissed his charming nature and suggested that it was a cover for his criminal activity. For Billy-in-the-Bowl was suspected of some very strange deeds in the locality.

As a beggar, he frequented markets, fairs and places where the public gathered, where he picked up a good deal of money. In these places, he behaved himself, and showed he knew his place by his talk and demeanour.

However, it was whispered, that there was a darker side to the laughing young man. They wondered if he knew anything about attacks on single women in the quiet lanes leading in and out of Dublin. Someone had taken to hiding in ditches and hedges on the lonely parts of the roads. There he waited until a suitable person was passing. Then, in a plaintive voice, he begged them to assist a poor, helpless man. Naturally enough, a person so addressed would stop to see what the poor man wanted. Sadly, that was their undoing.

Though he appeared to be only a half-man, Billy moved quickly enough to get the better of his victims, using his arms and strengthened torso to overpowering effect. He may not have had legs to run on, but he had enough body strength to overpower his victims, who in the main were women and likely not to possess his great strength. His victims were undone in one way or another and quickly relieved of anything of value. But this thief was different; for when he robbed his unsuspecting victims, he had no alternative but to do away with them to the great alarm of those who had to take this route home and knew not who or what lay in wait. He killed his victims to ensure their silence.

Ultimately, the beggar's undoing was his attempt to rob a pair of women who were passing near to where he lay, one fine day. According to reports of the time, the women had passed through Richardson's Lane, when they saw Billy at one of the stiles between fields. They said they suspected nothing untoward and were not displeased to have encountered such a fine man who seemed to need some assistance, which they were only too pleased to offer. Ordinary curiosity, together with Billy's coaxing and charming manner, induced them to approach him to examine how he managed to get about in his extraordinary means of transport. They even resolved to offer him some monetary assistance to help him enjoy life a little more. They expressed their admiration and sympathy for his resolve in making the most of his situation. Billy, for his part, was profuse in his praise of the fine ladies who had so mercifully come out of their way to see a poor prisoner of life. One of the ladies bent down to inspect Billy's conveyance a little closer, while the other prepared a small gratuity that she would drop discretely into his bowl. All the while, Billy's eyes were noting their gold watches, bracelets, and other valuables that ladies wore to reflect their station in life. With skill acquired from much practise, he attacked them, and, before they could react, he dragged them down to his level where all the advantage of their legs to run away with was swiftly annulled. This sudden change in their circumstance, from being benefactors to a poor invalided beggar, to lying on the ground while his hands were all over them searching, pulling and dragging until it was no longer possible to know where the assault was going to land next, left both women in a state of shock.

The insistent force he used to possess himself of their valuables rendered them powerless and helpless, at first. Nonetheless, people under attack can sometimes muster strength they did not know they had. At last, they began to struggle and call for help. Nobody was close enough to be of any assistance to them, so they would have to come to their own aid in order not to perish. Billy-in-the-Bowl rolled his reinforced bowl over one of the victims to keep her still while he robbed her companion. The woman saw that despite Billy's strength, the defect of his lower body gave the companions an advantage over him in manoeuvrability. She seized his curling locks with her hand and she thrust her thumb into one of Billy's eyes. Billy-in-the-Bowl, unused to such a formidable and forthright response to his aggression, roared with surprised pain, and relaxed his hold of the woman who sprang up and jumped away from his grasp. They quickly managed to back away from the maddened man's grasping range.

With their hair dishevelled, their ornaments broken and scattered, and their clothes ruined, the two ladies made their escape, abandoning all behind them. Billy-in-the-Bowl, now almost deprived of the sight of one of his eyes, was left in his bowl to lament what might have been, and to contemplate the certain punishment that now awaited him once the law came looking for him. The terrified women returned to their friends in Manor Street, and once they told their story, no time was lost in raising the alarm and pursuing the attacker who had committed this latest assault.

Billy hid himself behind a hedge in the next field in a vain attempt to avoid capture. He was soon detected and taken away by members of the newly formed Dublin Police which, in 1786, had replaced the old watchmen system. Most of the valuables taken from the ladies were picked up on the ground where the attack had taken place. Billy-in-the-Bowl was placed in a barrow and brought in disgrace to jail and trial in Green Street. Unusually for the time, he was not hanged for his crimes of murder, but was sentenced to hard labour for the remainder of his days on earth.

Billy-in-the-Bowl's days of charming his victims to death were over. Life returned to normal in the quiet lanes, but for long afterwards, few people would undertake the journey alone, for who knew what lay around the next corner. Be it man or half man, the story of Billy-in-the-Bowl meant that caution was called for on the journey to the outskirts of Dublin City.

7

MATT TALBOT'S BED

Some people believe in the power of relics. Others have no time for them at all; they dismiss them as superstitious nonsense. There was a man in Dublin City who was a fervent believer in the relics of one particular holy man to whom he had a special devotion and he sold these relics to anyone that wanted one. To make them even more exclusive, he did not advertise that he had any such relics in his possession, much less that he would part with the odd one for a donation. A donation to what he never would say, but it was assumed he was speaking about a donating to some religious or charitable cause related to Matt Talbot, a decent and religious man that dropped dead in 1925 on a Dublin street on his way to early morning mass.

At this time, our friend Hatcha lived on Rutland Street Upper, the same street as Matt. Rutland Street was off Summerhill and the old Georgian houses were sub-divided. Just a few years earlier, at the time of the national headcount of 1911, there were six families sharing the house where Talbot lived. He shared his quarters with his mother who had brought him into the world when she was nineteen years old. She was by then seventy-six years old and had produced a dozen children, a not unusual number for the time. Talbot had not had much schooling before he began to seek work in the docks area, along with thousands of his contemporaries. The fortunate ones would be hired at the factory gate for a morning's or a day's work. Once work slowed down, such workers were dismissed or just not hired at all. Poverty reigned supreme.

Matt went to work in a wine merchant's store, a bad place for anyone who had a liking for alcohol. Before long, he was sampling the wares in the wine store and had started a love affair with drink that was to endure for many a day. In time, he left to work in the Custom House Dock with its warehouses filled with goods of all descriptions, including bonded whiskey.

Before mechanisation was introduced to handling of a ship's cargo, gangs of men unloaded and loaded lorries that came and went with barrels, boxes, bales, kegs and chests of all sorts of goods, destined for docking or departing ships. To be a fully paid worker in Custom House Dock, you had to have arrived at the age of majority. If you were younger than twenty-one, you were paid what was termed 'Boy's Wages', in other words, a pittance. Talbot was put to work in the whiskey stores. Before long, he was a confirmed alcoholic. He spent whatever wages he received and ran up debts besides wherever he could get credit.

This way of life went on for a further sixteen years, until, one day, Talbot decided to become a teetotaller following a cathartic moment of self-realisation. He was to embrace sobriety for the remaining forty years of his life. He began to attend daily mass, and to repay his debts to those he could find to whom he owed money.

By the time the 1913 lockout of workers began in Dublin, when employers locked out workers for seeking better conditions and pay, Talbot was working in the huge timber yard of T&C Martin in the docks. The men in T&C Martin found themselves on the workers' side. A union member, Talbot gave his strike pay to other workers that he considered to be in poorer circumstances than he. He continued to live alone in a small room with very little furniture after his mother's death in 1915. He slept on a plank bed with a piece of timber for a pillow. He rose at 5 a.m. every day to attend mass, before walking on to work. On Sundays he attended several masses.

Appropriately perhaps for a holy man, he dropped dead on the public street on Granby Lane on 7 June on his way to mass in the Dominican church on Dominick Street. After his sudden demise it was discovered that Talbot was a religious zealot. He wore chains under his clothing to mortify his flesh in pursuit of personal excellence. People began to pray to him for intercession in their own lives. His coffined remains may be seen to this day in his parish church on Sean McDermott Street. Lots of Dublin people still pray to him for help with whatever troubles them in their daily lives.

However there were two camps: those that thought him mad to be doing such a thing to himself and those that thought him a saintly man who was even now in heaven and who could intercede with God in particular cases, if asked civilly and properly.

Hatcha was a non-believer, but saw no reason whatsoever not to benefit from the excitement and wonder of it all. After all, God helps those who help themselves. People began calling to the street to see the place where Talbot lived. Hatcha, being an entrepreneur before the word was ever coined, took it upon himself to be the liaison officer for the street. Those who believed Talbot to be the real thing were happy with any information that Hatcha and his pals could give them. Most of it was made up, for Talbot had been too enthusiastic about his prayerfulness and early mass for a lot of them to bother with him. Many on the street preferred to lie abed until the streets were well aired.

By and by, Hatcha noticed that people were touching the street railings that ran along the front of the old three-storey over-basement house that were put there to prevent people from falling down to the basement level below. He asked a few of them why they were doing that. They replied they were saying a silent prayer to Matt Talbot for their own intentions, meaning they were asking him for something they could not get themselves.

It was only a short step from there for Hatcha to say he had acquired the plank that his old friend Matt used to sleep on along with the pillow. He had been successfully treating them for woodworm, he said, of which there was a lot about in the days before science began eradicating them; so people would readily accept this as a reason for his possessing a dead man's bed. Sadly, he said quietly, poor Matt no longer had any use for either, having gone to his eternal rest where all the pillows were made of clouds and the beds of pink and white marshmallows.

He would take a while to allow the penny to drop with his listener. He would even walk away up towards Great Charles Street at the upper end of Rutland Street as if he was heading around into Mountjoy Square on important business. He never got further than the nearest gas lamp on Rutland Street before his sleeve would be caught by his hurrying companion. 'Would there be any chance of getting the bed or the pillow maybe or even a lend of one or the other for the night?' he might be asked. He would allow that it would be good if he could, but sadly such had been the extent of the damage caused by the Devil's little helpers in the woodworm that there was not a whole lot left. He'd ask then what the supplicant had in mind for the aforementioned. Inevitably, it would be as a relic to apply to a troubled area or to be placed beneath the pillow of a sufferer in the hope of a cure. Hatcha would ask whether if a small piece of the pillow would suffice. If so, he could easily slice a sliver off and let the person have it for cost price, seeing as how it was for as good a cause as Matt had stood for when he was alive, even though he had not lived to settle up with Hatcha for the work undertaken against the woodworm. No sooner said than done, and the delighted admirer of the late Matt Talbot parted company with their cash.

Hatcha started off a chain of customers, as word spread of the secret of the relics of Matt Talbot. Business took off so well that Hatcha was hard set to keep up with the demand for more and more relics of his late neighbour. He did not, of course, have possession of anything at all that had belonged to Talbot, nor did he even know where his few bits of furniture had gone to after his death. They had most likely been purloined for firewood by someone else. Hatcha, you see, had taken an old wooden wardrobe belonging to his late uncle and had chopped it into smithereens in the back garden of his own house. These bits he then sold – with the sharpness planed off them in case anyone was injured by accident – as bits of Talbot's plank bed.

Many is the happy man that brought home a bit of Hatcha's uncle's wardrobe and persuaded his wife to pray over it for their good intentions, mostly relating to drink problems. Many is the wife who doubted it did any good at all, but who muttered away over the bit of wood sitting on top of the chest of drawers, in the hope that it might keep her man a little closer to home, in future. Just as the enthusiastic Hatcha was thinking of hiring a few sub-contractors on the far side of the city to help him with his thriving business, it all came tumbling down around him.

When he had run out of chopped wood from his uncle's wardrobe, he started going to the auction rooms along Bachelors Walk and Ormond Quay. He placed bids on a wardrobe every week and brought each home in the dark of the evening on a borrowed handcart. His end came on a night when he stopped for a drink on Parnell Street and parked the cart with the wardrobe around the corner. When he came out, he saw that someone had stolen the handcart and had left the wardrobe standing there against the wall, as it was unsuited to the requirements of whatever the job was the handcart was now engaged upon.

There was nothing for it but to put the wardrobe up on his back and to walk up Summerhill, like a snail with his house upon his back. Small children soon started to follow him asking if he was going to live inside the wardrobe or was he going to rent it out for dances. Once children gathered, adults took notice of the strange sight of a red-faced Hatcha struggling home with the wardrobe. The game was finally up when he turned the corner into the street and found there was a queue of people there waiting for their promised relics. Hatcha put down the wardrobe and said he would be back in a while and left them to it.

Some people believe in the power of relics while other people have no time for them at all. Hatcha had no intention of being the referee when the ructions started over where the relics of Matt Talbot came from in the first place and whether he was a saint or a madman. It was enough to drive any one to drink. Hatcha had no view on that, one way or another. He was off to find the handcart thief and to have a word with him.

8

ARCHBISHOP O'HURLEY BECOMES A GHOST

Many people will be familiar with the part of Dublin where an archbishop used to read the Canon of the Mass in the years following his public hanging. It is not so far away on Gallows Green, where modern Baggot Street now lies and where the ghosts of victims past must surely linger to this day.

Witnesses reported that on dark and stormy nights, the ghost of the archbishop, dressed in the mourning vestments of the time, was to be seen reading by a pale light on a phantom altar raised over his grave in St Kevin's Cemetery on Camden Row. It was said that, during the mass, when the ghost came to the raising of the Host, the lights flickered out and the altar was nowhere to be seen.

The people of Dublin made pilgrimage to his grave to pray for many years after his ignominious execution. Archbishop Dermot O'Hurley, a Limerick man, was hanged in 1584 when the Penal Laws were in force and Queen Elizabeth I was the supreme head of the Protestant Church in Britain and Ireland. The Penal Laws were a series of measures imposed to discriminate against Roman Catholics and Protestant dissenters in favour of the established Church of Ireland. It was a treasonable offence to refuse to acknowledge the English monarch as head of the Church. Many Catholics who refused to do so were put to death as a result of this.

Under such restrictions, visits to the grave of a dead Catholic Archbishop were fraught with danger for the prayerful. Attendance gradually fell away until the practice of praying there died off altogether and the grave and its troubled occupant were left in peace.

Dermot O'Hurley was born in County Limerick in the early sixteenth century. Once grown to manhood, he went to the Continent to undergo the necessary training to become a priest. He resided in Belgium for fifteen years, where he was appointed Professor at Louvain, following his ordination. He held the chair of Canon Law at Rheims for four years. In 1581, whilst he was at Rome, he was appointed to be Archbishop of Cashel.

In those penal days of both severe and petty restriction, Catholic churchmen had to travel in disguise for their personal safety. O'Hurley opted to travel alone to avoid spies and informers who wanted to benefit by unmasking any priest they could find to the authorities. A bishop would carry a fine reward for the informer. O'Hurley was particularly cautious on his return to his native land not to be apprehended. For added security, his papers and everything to do with his new job were sent as cargo in another ship. As fortune would have it, the second ship was taken by pirates. But the pirates were themselves taken in by the authorities.

The Papal Bulls declaring O'Hurley's consecration as a bishop, his letters of introduction, and all his documentation were produced in evidence against him when he himself appeared as a prisoner, in court in Dublin. Earlier, on arrival in Ireland, O'Hurley travelled quietly to Waterford. But he was recognised, captured, and placed in prison to be interrogated. He managed to escape and moved up the country to continue his work.

He travelled to Carrick-on-Suir, where he was welcomed by the Earl of Ormond. However, while he was sheltering at Slane Castle he was seized by Thomas Fleming, Baron of Slane, and in chains was brought to Dublin. It was said his sufferings on the road were intense and that every indignity and hardship possible was inflicted upon him by his captors. Lodged securely in chains in Dublin Castle, O'Hurley was brought before Loftus, the Protestant Archbishop of Dublin, and Sir Henry Wallop, for examination. He freely told his interrogators that he was a priest of Rome, and an archbishop, to boot. The captured cleric was confined in a dark, dismal, and fetid dungeon in the Birmingham Tower, at the centre of the castle. He was kept in chains there until the following year while interrogations went on. Despite a long series of examinations, no crime was discovered against him, other than having a different faith to that of the established church.

In frustration, Wallop ordered that O'Hurley be subjected to the 'Boots Torture', in the hope that if he could not extort a confession from him, then he might force him to deny his professed faith and to embrace Protestantism. It is recorded in *Collins Chapters of Old Dublin* that the executioner placed the archbishop's feet and calves in tin boots filled with a mixture of salt, bitumen, oil, tallow, pitch, and boiling water through which ran small streams of boiling oil. They fastened his feet in wooden shackles or stocks, and placed fire under them. The boiling oil penetrated the feet and legs so deeply that morsels of skin and flesh fell off and left the bones bare.

If the officials of the government gathered there in the Castle Yard hoped that this torture would turn O'Hurley's beliefs around, they were mistaken. During all his agony, the archbishop did not cry out beyond praying that Jesus,

Son of David, would have mercy upon him. Even this sear-
ing torture could not wring a confession of falsehood from
him. Finally, an exhausted O'Hurley lay on the ground, just
short of death but in such a way that the executioner feared
he had exceeded his orders of torture to confession. He had
the victim carefully removed from the apparatus and taken
back to his cell where he received medical treatment for his
appalling injuries.

In time, the archbishop recovered to face another danger
concocted by his tormentors. Both Loftus and Wallop were
to be replaced in office by Sir John Perrot. There was to be
a formal ceremony of handing over the sword of office as
power passed from the pair. Loftus and Wallop thinking
that the new regime would release O'Hurley, decided to try
him by court martial and have him condemned to death,
before they left office.

Loftus told the story two years later in his official report:

> We thought it meet, according to our direction, to proceed
> with him by court martial, and for our farewell, two days
> before we delivered over the sword, we gave warrant to the
> Knight Marshal, in his Majesty's name, to do execution on
> him, which accordingly was performed, and thereby the
> realm well rid of a most pestilent member. This occurred on
> the Friday preceding the installation of Perrot.

The archbishop, who could no longer walk because of the
injuries to his feet, was drawn on a hurdle through the castle
garden. He was taken away without any noise or fuss, such
was the haste of his arch-enemies in getting rid of him. They
may have feared that the people would raise a disturbance
and rescue their minister from death, if it were known that
he was to be executed. Loftus and Wallop ordered that he
be brought out of the castle before sunrise, and before the
people were up, to be hung on the public gallows, a distance
away from the seat of power in the castle.

It was said that only two townsmen met him as he was hauled on his way to the place of execution. This pair and William Fitzsimons, a friend of his, accompanied O'Hurley through his final journey to his public hanging. Archbishop O'Hurley was hanged near St Stephen's Green, which was then outside the city. The Green was then an osiery where rod-like willow was grown for the construction of houses of clay and wattle and for making baskets which were widely used at the time.

To prolong the condemned man's agony, his three executioners hanged him with a sort of noose made of sturdy interlaced willow twigs, the effect of which was to slowly strangle him rather than to hang him. It is said that the site of the public scaffold for executions was where modern Fitzwilliam Street crosses Baggot Street, known as Gallows Road, when O'Hurley and many more were put to death.

The bodies of the condemned were thrown into a trench beneath the scaffold following the execution and O'Hurley's dead body was thrown there to rot with the others. He was dead and could cause no further trouble to the high and the mighty and those with beliefs contrary to his. However, his friend William Fitzsimons had the remains of the martyr recovered and enclosed in a coffin. He saw to it that they were reinterred in a consecrated burial place. He had to wait until darkness had fallen before he had the remains brought to the old burial ground of St Kevin's, in Camden Row near the Meath Hospital where they were prayed over and laid to what was hoped a final rest. Although a Protestant cemetery, St Kevin's had come by custom to be used by Catholics and Quakers for burials. But if his tormentors thought that was the end of it, they were mistaken. No sooner was he dead than the song 'Slane's Treason' or 'The Fall of the Baron of Slane', was written and became widely known. It was set to music by Richard Cruise, the distinguished harper.

Followers of the archbishop made pilgrimage to his grave and people reported seeing his defiant ghost celebrating mass on nights when the elements rode wild over Dublin City. It seemed as if restitution was being sought from the heavens for an injustice. According to *Burke's 1879 History of the Irish Lord Chancellors*, 'Multitudes of pilgrims for three centuries thronged to his tomb, which the fancy, perhaps the superstition, of the people clothed with many legends.'

His body may have died, but the people of Dublin kept the Limerick man's memory alive in their hearts. He became one of the most celebrated of Irish Catholic martyrs, who chose to die rather than deny his convictions. Even in death, O'Hurley was never far from the heart of Dublin and its goings-on. At the start of the nineteenth century, St Kevin's cemetery became a target of the sack-'em-up body-snatchers. Determined action by the authorities apprehended the thieves and peace returned once more to this corner of Dublin.

Another Pope in Rome was to recognise the work of this singular man. Dermot O'Hurley was beatified by Pope John Paul II in September 1992 as one of seventeen Irish Catholic martyrs who died for their belief. The archbishop is commemorated in his native Limerick by the Archbishop O'Hurley Memorial Church in Caherline County Limerick. St Kevin's church closed in 1912. The old St Kevin's graveyard has been converted into a modern public park now hidden away on Camden Row near the busy Wexford Street. It is a place of peace, at last. There are no longer any reports of a hanged archbishop celebrating a ghostly mass over the grave of a man who gave up his life for his conviction.

9

SHERIDAN LE FANU'S GHOSTS OF CHAPELIZOD

One dark night in Chapelizod some years ago, a black dog that no one owned began to howl. He did not stop for many hours. It is still remembered chillingly by those who heard the disturbing dirge as it roiled around the small houses of the town. Some said it was just an unfortunate dog who was lost and was howling for its master to come to rescue it from the empty streets where nothing and nobody stirred. But others said it was a Banshee, in animal form, come to foretell the death of a chosen one.

It is said the Banshee only comes for someone from one of the great families of Ireland, those with names beginning with an 'O', as in O'Neill, O'Donnell, O'Brien. But many other families whose Anglicised names do not carry the 'O' nonetheless have an 'Ó' in Irish; Ó meaning descended from. So the Banshee could be calling for any Irishman, whose name is known only to the harbinger of death.

Few chose to leave their homes to seek the keener that night. Most pulled the curtains closed and left the night outside. Some prayed the visitation would pass their home by. Some knelt and made a sign of the cross while they prayed; others shrugged and kept their prayer private to themselves. Few slept easily in their bed until dawn came.

The following morning, the dog was nowhere to be seen, not on the streets of Chapelizod, not in Phoenix Park beside it, not on any of the roads leading to the town, nor in the surrounding parishes. It was as if the phantom had simply vanished. People asked one another what it could have been, but no one could say for certain what they had heard that night. In the natural order of life, some older people passed away in the weeks following that weeping through the streets, so who knew what happened to the soul that was destined to be taken that night. It was the sort of story that Chepelizod takes in its stride.

Sheridan Le Fanu lived in the Phoenix Park in the Royal Hibernian School during the first eleven years of his life. His father, Thomas Le Fanu, a Church of Ireland clergyman, was appointed to the chaplaincy of the school for orphaned and abandoned children of members of the British Army. Interested in the unexplained as he was, Sheridan Le Fanu made sure to feature Phoenix Park and Chapelizod in his stories of Gothic horror. He was called to the bar in 1839, but abandoned law for journalism, newspaper ownership and ghost stories, some of which were told in such detail about Chapelizod that their footsteps may still be followed by late-night wanderers to this day.

In 1851, *Dublin University Magazine* published his *Ghost Stories of Chapelizod*, a collection of three stories: 'The Village Bully', 'The Sexton's Adventure', and 'The Spectre Lovers'.

In 'The Spectre Lovers', Peter Brien leaves nearby Palmerstown, in the early hours of the morning, with a head full of drink, to return to his grandmother's house where he lives. He pauses on the bridge over the Liffey. Upstream, as he watches, small houses begin to appear on the bank of the river behind the town's Main Street. He wonders why he has never seen them before, and wanders around into the Square.

To his horror, he sees a troop of soldiers, dressed in uniforms of a bygone age, marching towards their barracks with terror on their faces at what might be following behind. Le Fanu describes it as a column of foot-soldiers, marching with perfect regularity, and headed by an officer on horseback. As they pass by, Peter falls into step with an officer. He leads him to an old ivy-covered house beside the graveyard. The house has a green door with a bright brass knocker on it.

There they meet a young woman in an upstairs room, keening for her lost treasure. She and the officer point to a stone sill and say the treasure is there. When Peter looks to where they point, he sees, to his horror, a small baby smiling back at him with outstretched arms. Instead of accepting the child's embrace he faints at the enormity of it all. He recovers consciousness on the ground outside. He sees that the house has returned to its familiar derelict state.

His grandmother tells him that what he saw was the ghost of the Royal Irish Regiment that was garrisoned in Chapelizod. An old neighbour tells him he saw the ghost of Captain Deveraux at the house. Deveraux was said to be responsible for a young woman's ruin and death. The twist in the tale comes when Peter goes climbing about on the top of the ruined building to see if he can find real treasure. He falls and dies and is buried in the graveyard along with everyone else involved in the story.

The story of 'The Village Bully' relates the tale of Bully Larkin who challenges Long Ned Moran to a fistfight at the top of Barney's Hill. Larkin sets his sights on a young woman who likes Ned better. When Ned yields to the Bully's taunts, Larkin beats him so badly that Ned later dies from his injuries. However, it is just a little too long afterwards for a charge of murder to be brought against Larkin. Some time later, on a moonlit night, as Larkin returns from his work, across the park and starts down the hill for home, a long, lean figure climbs across the graveyard wall. It runs up the hill and accosts Larkin who falls down with the effects of a stroke, in shock. Larkin, in a twist of fate takes his own time to die. Not being able to work for a living, Larkin becomes destitute and relies on alms from the people he tormented in his prime. He is buried in the same graveyard alongside Long Ned Moran.

With two stories already set around the graveyard, Le Fanu features the cemetery in the third story: 'Sexton's Adventure'. The parish sexton, Bob Martin, drinks a good deal more punch than is good for his health and than is consistent with the good character of an ecclesiastical functionary. His thirst was such that at times he drops in on drinking friends who had forgotten to invite him to the drinking session. He misses no opportunity to attend wakes or anything else that passes for an excuse to consume drink. He befriends Phil Slaney, the proprietor of a public house on the road to the city, just outside the town of Chapelizod. It is near to where the old turnpike or toll gates stood on the road. Slaney does not drink alcohol to any great extent when the friendship begins. But such is Bob Martin's engaging company and store of stories and gossip that the publican begins matching the sexton drink for drink and before long is a drunkard himself.

Then, as Le Fanu describes it:

> One drowsy summer morning, the weather being at once sultry and cloudy, Phil Slaney goes into a small back parlour, where he keeps his books, and which commands, through its dirty window-panes, a full view of a dead wall. He bolts the door, takes a loaded pistol, and claps the muzzle to his mouth. He blows the upper part of his skull through the ceiling.

This turn of events leads Bob Martin to foreswear drink altogether, that and a lack of invitations from other publicans to ensconce himself on their premises. Some time later, Bob Martin is sent for to receive instructions on a funeral that is to come to the graveyard. He is delayed and on his way home has to pass Phil Slaney's closed public house. To his surprise, he sees a man with a glass and a bottle of whiskey sitting outside, with a saddled horse beside him. The man beckons Bob Martin over, but he declines, saying he has to be away home and anyway he no longer drinks alcohol.

The man follows him in the darkness waving the bottle and the glass at him. The horse walks along behind him. The man is dressed for a journey with a riding coat and a hat upon his head. In the darkness, Bob can not see his face beneath the brim of his hat. Bob hurries along and the man hurries after him. As soon as Bob arrives at his house, he bangs on the plank door in terror to be allowed in.

The man flings the glass at him but instead of liquid coming towards him, Bob sees only flame that seems to want to destroy him. The door opens behind him but not before a gust of wind blows away the stranger's hat, and the sexton beholds that his skull is roofless. Like poor Peter in the first story, Bob Martin falls down senseless, this time into his own doorway.

The following morning, when daylight comes to his door, Bob Martin and his wife see the old thorn tree beside the door was burnt during the night. Whether it was lightning that struck it during an overnight storm, or an angry Phil Slaney come to take Bob Martin away on the horse on a ride to Hell, we don't know.

Just as we don't know why a howling dog came down the Main Street of Chapelizod seeking someone still unnamed when all of the good people of that town stayed inside with doors firmly locked. For it is better to remain indoors when terror stalks the streets of Chapelizod that old, old, village on the outskirts of Dublin city.

10

REVD JACKSON DEAD IN THE DOCK FOR A DAY

Some strange things happen in Dublin from time to time. At the end of the eighteenth century, a man sat in a Dublin dock awaiting sentence for treason. Plenty of others had sat there before him, on the way to their judicially prescribed death. This man was unusual in that his head was on fire while the judge made ready his sentencing address.

This state of affairs did not last long for the Revd William Jackson expired before the judge could pass sentence on him. Jackson's head was seen by a witness to be smoking when he removed his hat. And so this man of the cloth and later the pen denied Lord Clonmel the opportunity of sentencing him to anything other than a Christian burial.

Events took an even more bizarre twist, when the judge ordered that the body should remain where it was until an inquest could be carried out on the death of this supposed Irish revolutionary and French spy.

Jackson's early life would not have suggested that such a bizarre turn of events was to lie in the future. Born in Newtownards, County Down, in 1737, Jackson studied at Oxford and was ordained a preacher. Although he gained some popularity as a preacher, he soon found that it was not a sustainable occupation. Instead, he took up journalism and partisan writing as a means of earning a living. Much of his subsequent life was given over to partisanship of one sort or another, operating as an eighteenth-century equivalent of a spin doctor to various causes and individuals in return for financial return. At one stage, he joined forces with the actor John Palmer to build a new theatre in the City of London. The pair persuaded investors to contribute more than £18,000 to the construction of the Royalty Theatre. However, they neglected to obtain Lord Chamberlain's authorisation for their first stage production and, as a consequence, the theatre closed after the opening night. Naturally, the investors initiated legal action against the partners, citing fraud by the pair.

Jackson fled to France, where he became involved in the revolutionary fervour that was sweeping that country. By 1793, Jackson was commissioned as a spy by the French. He was recruited to travel to England and Ireland to assess the Irish public's inclination towards armed revolution against the British. By the age of fifty-eight, he was in Dublin and met with Wolfe Tone and other United Irishmen. His task was to persuade the Irish that France would lend aid to their nationalist cause if they would rebel against the Crown.

The Society of United Irishmen wanted to end British rule over Ireland and establish an independent Irish republic. However, in passing through London on his way to Dublin, Jackson divulged his plans to John Cockayne, an old friend of his, and an attorney. Cockayne was not of Jackson's convictions, though he pretended to be. It was to be Jackson's undoing. Once Cockayne heard what was afoot, he entered into private communication with Prime Minister Pitt in London and informed him of the purpose of Jackson's visit to Dublin. He revealed everything that had passed between him and his friend. When Jackson left London for Dublin, he was accompanied by Cockayne. Following his meetings in Dublin with United Irishmen, Jackson sent a report by Wolfe Tone speaking about a possible rebellion, along with other letters, in the mail. These were seized by the authorities.

Jackson was arrested on a charge of high treason. He was to be tried a year later and convicted on Cockayne's evidence. The year-long delay was at his request, allowing him time to assemble a defence and to procure witnesses. It was all to no avail. On 23 April 1795, he was found guilty and was to be sentenced to death by Lord Clonmel. However, Jackson determined that he would end his life in his own way.

He is said to have enjoyed breakfast with his second wife on that fateful morning. Jackson had lost his first wife to breast cancer in the early 1770s. What happened next is told in *Gilbert's Streets of Dublin* which was published in the 1850s, many years after the event, though it was still spoken about in Dublin, for it is not too often that a prisoner dies in the dock. Rarer still does it occur by the defendant's own hand. He took poison that morning, possibly supplied by his wife. When he removed his hat in court, one observer noted that steam or smoke immediately rose from his head. He was not at all well, most people agreed, and he did not look well. His health deteriorated while Chief Justice Lord Clonmel was speaking.

The convicted man's condition worsened more as his lawyers made detailed and wide-ranging speeches, hoping to save their client the worst of sentencing. They were trying to keep their client alive while he was intent on killing himself. The judge was impatient to pass sentence of death on him. So ill did Jackson become, that a chair was brought for him to sit on while he suffered the pangs of pain which were wracking his entire body. Such was his evident distress, that it was proposed by the defence that he should be remanded, as he was in a state of health that rendered any communication between him and his counsel impracticable.

However, the Chief Justice was in a hurry to sentence the dying man. It was pointed out that Jackson was, by then, in a state of insensibility, which left the court in a quandary. Clonmel, stating the blinding obvious, said it was impossible to pronounce the judgment of the court upon him while he was in that condition. Nonetheless, Thomas Kinsley, one of the jurors, offered to physically examine the Revd Jackson to see how he was. This was agreed to by all concerned, with the exception of one defendant who was past giving permission for anything.

Kinsley went into the dock with Jackson, and in a short time informed the court that in his opinion the prisoner was certainly dying. Clonmel ordered that Kinsley be sworn in to ensure the evidence being given was truthful, just in case. Once he was duly sworn, Clonmel asked Kinsley if he was in any profession that might give authority to his opinion on the health of the prisoner. Kinsley replied that he was an apothecary. Clonmel, still intent on passing sentence, asked if Jackson was capable of hearing the judgment. Kinsley said he did not think he could. Lord Clonmel ordered that Jackson be taken away, and that care be taken that no mischief be done to him. Revd Jackson was to be remanded until further orders of the court. Under the circumstances, Clonmel said, it was as much for the defendant's advantage as for anyone else's to adjourn the hearing.

However, the Sheriff now informed the court that the prisoner was in fact dead. Given this turn of events, Lord Clonmel ordered that an inquest be held on the body. He wanted to know by what means Revd Jackson had died. The Court made to adjourn, but as Clonmel was retiring from the bench to his chamber, the Sheriff inquired how he should act with regard to the dead body. His lordship, without pausing in his progress, replied that he should act as is usual in such cases; as if prisoners expired in the dock, with their wigs on fire, on a regular basis. His comment was interpreted to mean that the corpse should stay where it was. The body of the deceased therefore remained in the dock, unmoved from the position, in which its owner had expired. It stayed there until the following day, when an inquest was held.

It was found that, on his way to court that morning, Jackson had reportedly vomited out of the carriage window, suggesting that something was amiss before his head ever started to steam in court. An autopsy on the corpse found that Jackson had ingested a large quantity of a metallic poison. The suggestion was that it had been administered by his wife, but she was never proceeded against for such a crime, though she could have been said to have benefitted from the sudden demise of her husband. The effect of his suicide was that, since he had not been sentenced for treason by the court, his family could inherit his goods, and a pension to boot.

The remains of the Revd Jackson were brought to St Michan's church on Church Street and buried in the graveyard there. His resting place was close to the church, underneath which are the mummified remains of several people, preserved by the unique atmosphere in the limestone vaults. Among the remains are a 100-year-old nun; a very large man, popularly believed to have been a crusader; a body with its feet and right hand severed; and the Sheares brothers, Henry and John, who took part in the 1798 rebellion. A suitable collection of silent companions for the man that cheated the court out of taking his life away from him by voluntarily giving up his own life.

Interred in the same graveyard as Jackson is Oliver Bond, a leader of the United Irishmen, whom Jackson in all probability had met. Bond also cheated the Crown of its punishment of him for his activities. Bond was arrested in 1798 and sentenced to death. Like Jackson, he was defended by John Philpot Curran and George Ponsonby, eminent men in their day. His sentence was commuted, but within five weeks he died suddenly of apoplexy. These men certainly had a lot to talk about, wherever they all ended up in the afterlife. Especially when Clonmel joined them in their new abode. We can but hope that it was not a place where heads on fire is so normal a sight that no one remarks on it.

11

St Valentine

Say what you like, but it's hard to claim that St Valentine is actually a Dubliner. For that you would need to be either born in the city, or to have lived in Dublin long enough to seem like you are a local. Having your bones brought to Dublin by a priest, on his way home from a business trip, is not quite the same thing.

This is supposed to have happened to St Valentine's remains, which are now venerated in Dublin. However, there are other cities that claim to posses the remains of the patron saint of lovers. Maybe his bones were separated and everyone has a part of him. Or maybe there may have been umpteen Valentines in existence, so when they all died, their bones could have been spread around the world, so fretting lovers could seek their intercession in matters romantic. Whoever he was, the feast of St Valentine was established in 496 by Pope Gelasius I, who included Valentine among those whose names are justly reverenced among men, but whose acts are known only to God. Which is what love seems to be at times: something reverenced by man but known only to God.

To cast even more doubt on the Valentine legend, the official feast day was deleted from the Roman calendar of saints in 1969 by Pope Paul VI, when he ordered a cull of uncertain saints. The 14 February feast day of St Valentine was officially relegated to calendars of local or national interest at that time. So, while the day is celebrated in many countries, it is no longer recognised as a feast day by his official church.

On that day each year, many loving couples attend Whitefriar Street church to visit the shrine there of St Valentine, wherein his bones are said to lie. And the story of how they got to be there goes like this …

John Spratt was a gifted Irish preacher and a Master of Sacred Theology of the Order of Calced Carmelites when he visited Rome in 1835. His speaking style attracted praise, and many of his listeners were moved to present him with gifts of appreciation when he had finished speaking. Pope Gregory XVI gave the best gift of all. He gave John the supposed remains of St Valentine to bring home to Dublin to his order: the Whitefriar Street Carmelites. Not wishing to be excommunicated for saying no to a pope, John brought his new possession home with him to Dublin, where it has been ever since.

His modern-day order offers the following explanation of what happened. When the bones arrived in Dublin they were accompanied by a letter from the powers that be in the Vatican. It said that the Vatican certified and attested that it had freely given to the Very Revd Fr Spratt the blessed body of St Valentine. Furthermore, it said that on 27 December 1835, the remains were taken out of the cemetery of St Hippolytus in the Tiburtine Way, Rome, together with a small vessel said to be tinged with St Valentine's blood. They were deposited in a wooden case covered with painted paper. They were then tied with a red silk ribbon and sealed with papal seals.

Fr Lucas was granted permission to transmit the remains beyond Rome and then to expose and place the blessed holy body for the public veneration of the faithful in any church, oratory or chapel. By November of the following year, 1836, the reliquary containing the remains had arrived in Dublin and was brought in solemn procession to the church where it was received by Archbishop Murray of Dublin. People then began making pilgrimage there and praying for love to shine upon them. However, once Fr Spratt departed this world himself in 1871 at the age of seventy-six, following a lifetime of work among Dublin's poor, public interest in the relics died away and they were placed in storage.

However, midway through the twentieth century, more than 100 years after they were first brought to Dublin, they were returned to prominence, when an altar and shrine were constructed to house them and to enable them to be viewed once more. Acknowledging that establishing absolute provenance of the remains would be difficult the authorities say, 'The Reliquary contains some of the remains of St Valentine – it is not claimed that all of his remains are found in this casket.' The small vessel tinged with the blood of the martyr is included according to the order.

The casket is housed in a larger outer casket and is in view beneath the side altar for most of the year. The outer casket has only been opened to verify that the contents are intact. The inner box has not been opened or the seals broken, according to the order. Valentine's Day is the big day when the reliquary is removed from beneath a side-altar and placed before the high altar in the church. A short Blessing of Rings for those about to be married is conducted at masses on that day. Valentine's Day is linked with an old belief that birds are supposed to pair off and become lovers on or about that day in mid-February. While Christmas Day is a day for the family, New Year's Day is for new beginnings, St Valentine's Day is a day for love and lovers.

It was natural then for Tom from Irishtown to think of proposing on that day. He had been in Whitefriar Street church a few weeks earlier and was taken with the concept that the patron saint of lovers was just a few feet away from where he sat in the smooth pew. Tom rarely bothered with love and the like in real life. He was a film addict and pre-

ferred his experiences of life at a distance in darkened cinema. Mousie, on the other hand, never went to the cinema. Her baptismal name was Margaret though she was never called that. It was a while now since she had been a blushing maiden and had decided this year that she would rather have one bird in the hand than many in the bush. She began to think about a likely life companion for herself.

She liked Tom who came into her bicycle shop now and then to have his bicycle repaired. He was always polite and grateful and paid whatever the tariff was without comment, even when he knew she had added a little over the odds to the bill because she knew he would not complain.

Tom for his part, had eyes for Betty who ran a craft shop down the street. But Betty wasn't fussed about Tom, though she knew that his late mother was rumoured to have won a tidy sum on the lottery. If she did, she had never spent a penny of it, so it was likely Tom was a wealthy man. Apart from visits to the cinema, Tom liked to watch sales channels on television. It was while watching an exciting jewellery presentation on a buy-now sales channel that he made a decision that would change his life. He would propose to Betty on St Valentine's Day and see what she'd have to say about that.

They had never been on a date. Or, for that matter, had they ever conducted a conversation of any great length. To Tom's way of thinking, this was to his advantage, for there would be no past misunderstandings to be rid of before they began their new life together. So he picked out a nice pair of earrings on a TV show for Betty's engagement present. He suspected there might have been something wrong with his television when the earrings arrived in the post a week later. They would have rattled around inside a matchbox with space to spare, they were that small. But the sellers had filled up the package with lots of nice soft tissue. Suppressing his disappointment, Tom thought a nice necklace would set the earrings off nicely.

As for a ring, Betty could choose a ring herself in the jeweller's later on when they had decided to tell people about their engagement. Come the big day, St Valentine's Day, Tom was sporting a new haircut and went past Betty's busy craft shop several times without going in. He had the earrings and the necklace ready in his pocket but anytime he looked into the shop, Betty was dealing with another customer.

At this point, he thought better of his original plan of just walking in and putting the question to her. She might not hear him. Best to leave it until she was closed and she was at home. It would be more special then: private, romantic even. That was the plan, but like many a suitor before him, his St Valentine's Day venture came unstuck.

He called to the house. He rang the bell. Before it was answered he heard a voice inside that surprised him and almost made him run away. Tom was sure that Betty lived alone, so who was the older man standing before him who had answered the door?

'Can I help you?' asked the man.

'Is she there herself?' Tom asked, playing for time.

'If you're here for my daughter, you had better come in while she gets ready.' Later Tom learned that the man was the girl's father, returned from a long stay in another country but back now to look after her. In the long years afterwards, Tom wondered how he had not noticed bits of bicycles lying about the house before it went too far. Betty, whom he had determined to propose to, was a craft worker and unless she was delivering her cottages of straw on her bike, this was not Betty's house and this was not her father. Too late.

By then, they had progressed in the conversation to the subject of Tom proposing to the man's daughter on this special night of the year. The man said he would approve of the marriage and when Mousie suddenly appeared in the doorway, Tom didn't have the heart to tell anyone that he was in the wrong house and about to propose to the wrong woman. So, he let St Valentine guide him.

Things turned out alright in the end. Tom never had to pay to have his bike repaired again, once they were safely married. Mousie's father helped Tom spend all of Tom's mother's hidden cash and Betty up the road went on making artefacts for sale while she waved to Tom as he walked slowly past her shop on most days of the year, St Valentine's Day included. Some relics are hard to lose. Tom has never returned to the church on Whitefriar Street to say a prayer. No point really.

12

MOLLY MALONE

Dubliners very rarely let the facts get in the way of a good story. For instance, the best English in the world is spoken in Dublin, according to most Dubliners. It is therefore a source of mystery to most of them why other English speakers cannot readily understand them and why Dublin-English is not recognised as the pre-eminent form of the language. It's the same when it comes to a good story. It matters not what its origin may have been; if it sounds good then it is good and will be told as truth. How else could you explain why Dubliners sing about a fishmonger of doubtful provenance, as if she were a first cousin on the mammy's granny's side a few years back. Or even why the city council decided to erect a memorial to a street seller of fish, who probably never existed, on the city's most prominent and fashionable street in the year 1988 that celebrated Dublin's millennium. A birth certificate was even produced during the millennium celebrations. There was a baptism in July 1663 in St John's Church of Ireland parish, of a baby girl of that name, more or less. Actually, the name recorded is of a Mary Malone. But sure it's close enough for a folk tale.

Dubliners like a good argument, so there were some who said that this was proof positive of the existence of a seventeenth-century fish seller being in the city. It was proof that someone was born and baptised, right enough, but it was a little optimistic to claim that it was proof of Molly's existence. There were others who were sure that Molly was a nineteenth-century person. Almost inevitably, there were those who said she was neither one nor the other for she was only a girl in a nice song about her mammy and daddy dying of a fever before their time and of their daughter following in their footsteps into the next life. There were also people who suggested that the sixteenth-century Molly might have been the great-something granny of the nineteenth-century girl. This makes sense if the business was in fact a family enterprise passed down through the generations as the song clearly states.

While Molly Malone is famed in the song that relates her supposedly short but tragic life on the streets of Dublin, a darker side has crept into the folk tale over the years. Some claim that as well as selling fish, Molly was a streetwalker selling her charms for money. But they are two incompatible occupations, for one involves late nights and the other early mornings.

The city's fish market, on a different side of the river to where her statue is now anchored, opened in the 1890s. Molly would have come here as a purveyor of cockles and mussels. In the age before refrigeration, it would have been necessary for Molly to be at the market very early. It seems like a long stretch then to suggest that she was also selling her feminine wares on the streets of the city through the night, for few prostitutes were tolerated on the streets of daytime Dublin. Molly, if she existed, needed to sleep sometime.

Traders and hawkers of all sorts wandered the streets selling their wares. According to the song Molly was a fishmonger, as were her parents before her. That much is common to all the stories of Molly Malone. They died of a fever, we are told, and Molly followed them in due course. But there is not much of a surprise there since the tight-knit houses and streets of Dublin were easy conduits for infections and fevers of all sorts.

Still, nowhere in the song is there any reference to her supposed nocturnal ramblings as her alter ego Molly Malone, good-time girl. If she did work in the world's oldest profession then she might have found herself as one of the attractions in the sporting houses of the Monto area of Dublin. Monto was a notorious red-light district in nineteenth and early twentieth-century Dublin, situated not far from the docks and the railway station on Amiens Street, now Connolly Station. It was estimated that some 1,600 women were working in the industry in the city at any time. One street was said to have some 200 young women working in brothels that were ruthlessly ruled over by madams and their fancy men enforcers. Some worked in Monto all the time and men came to them, while others travelled around the city's fashionable meeting places to find their clients and to bring them to the kips of Monto where the men were as likely to be robbed of their wallets as anything else. Disease was rife among the women in a time of indifferent sanitation or hygienic practice. That may have lead to the inference that Molly did not die of a fever or of tuberculosis, but of a venereal disease of some sort or other. Though how this can be construed from the song that is sung all over the world is a leap into the unknown.

If a working woman did appear to be at death's door with such a condition, she was brought to the Westmoreland Lock Hospital on Townsend Street. The lock hospitals specialised in the treatment of sexually transmitted disease. When opened first they treated both men and women. But, from 1820 onwards, only females were admitted to Townsend Street. Males were sent to Dr Steevens' Hospital in the west and the Richmond Hospital in the north of the city.

With so many British soldiers garrisoned in Dublin at the time, and many single men using the services of prostitutes, the authorities were anxious that communicable diseases be protected against as much as possible. Hopelessly affected women were transferred from the hospital to a Lock prison and kept there out of harm's way until their life ended. It is unlikely that Molly met her end there. For she seemed to be an entrepreneur of the finest kind, selling her cockles and mussels to all and sundry on the streets of her home town.

There is a monument to her on Grafton Street. Although the cart depicted in the monument is a hand cart and not a barrow, and her low-cut dress would cause her to contract pneumonia in Dublin's moist climate, Molly it seems, is in Dublin to stay. One thing is sure, she is already generating more Dublin folk tales just by standing there in all weathers, rain or shine, like a true Dublin street seller. For a start, she was conferred with the soubriquet of the Tart with the Cart, though few enough citizens actually call her that, preferring instead to call it the Molly Malone Statue. The actual sculpture was commissioned by Dublin City Council in their millennium year of 1988. The commission was granted in July of that year to the sculptor Jeanne Rynhart for completion and installation by late December. To guarantee a perfect result in the limited time-scale available, two heads were simultaneously prepared from the original mould. Both castings were successful.

Some twenty-three years later, in June 2011, the spare head of Molly Malone, a bronze bust measuring 22in by 15in, was offered for sale at auction in a Castlecomer art salesroom with a guide price of between €20,000 and €30,000. It was not sold on the day. So, not only is Molly said to have lived in two different centuries or not at all, her statue has a spare head, for the time when she might lose the head she has, if the argument goes on for much longer.

One thing is certain, the sound of the song being sung is like a homing beacon for Dubliners, who don't really care about the facts, but enjoy a song about one of their own. Molly Malone, whether she existed or not in the seventeenth or the nineteenth century, is alive-alive-o in the city of Dublin and wherever Dubliners gather together to explain how it is that they speak the best English in the world.

13

WAKES AND HEADLESS COACHMEN

In the olden times, people in Dublin told stories at wakes, to while away the hours before dawn and internment of the deceased. Poor people were generally buried without much fuss, while richer people were wont to show off their afflu-ence in big funerals, lots of carriages, respectful newspaper coverage and ostentatious memorials. But they were still as dead as the poor people.

Normally, when someone died, it was arranged to have a grave dug and a church service was organised to see off the dead person on their way to the next world. Nowadays, the corpse is generally brought to a funeral home where viewing of the remains is facilitated. In older times, people could not afford such luxury and the person was laid out in their own home with the assistance of neighbours who were versed in the niceties of respect for the dead. Stories were shared of other wakes where strange occurrences were seen in the night.

It was said that in parts of Dublin a phantom coach drawn by black horses would come galloping along the street. It would stop outside the wake house and take away any living soul unfortunate enough to be standing there, or fool-ish enough to wait about for such a thing to happen. Few people could attest to seeing the coach in reality, for if you had, you would be dead yourself. This story was circulated especially by the sack-'em-ups, as it had the great benefit of keeping people inside the house, where the curtains were already closed out of respect for the recently deceased, and where mirrors were turned to the wall. Closed curtains and empty streets helped the grave robbers to pass along with fresh bodies stolen from any cemetery that had seen a recent interment. This story carried on even when the grave robbers had gone to their own judgement, for a good story will outlast its first telling.

Such considerations matter very little to a man in love with a recently bereaved widow woman. In fact, the ceremonials and sombreness of death can heighten desire, as Andrew was to observe in his amorous pursuit of a dead man's wife.

Andrew was in love with the recently-bereaved Belinda, who was not paying him an awful lot of attention, on account of the death of her husband Tom. She had been married to Tom for more years than she had thought possible on her wedding day. Tom was a great deal older then she, but, as Tom would joke when demanding she join him on their knees in prayer every night, there was never any prospect of her catching up with him. Belinda did not believe in any religion but she dutifully followed her husband in his nightly devotions because she worked out that if she lived for another five years, and her husband did the same, then she would be rich, for he would surely expire on or before then.

There was neither chick nor child to be considered in disbursement of his fortune. The fortune, which he kept in a box of money beneath their bed, would be Belinda's and she would be young enough to enjoy it still. In fact, the fortune was the only reason that Belinda had married the man who was as old as her own father. He had come calling to her house when he was growing unsteady on his peasant legs, and needed someone to keep his house neat and tidy, and to prepare his food when he needed it. Belinda, who was not blessed with conventional beauty, agreed to marry him.

So excited was Tom at the prospect, that he ordered a very large candle from the candlemaker with their names embossed in gold, deep into the wax. He lit this candle every night of their married life, when they knelt down in prayer. In turn, the candle was the recipient of all her disappointment as she watched it flicker before her eyes every evening before the dreary hours of wheezing bed.

There are people living in Ireland who say that when the evil eye is put upon you, you will die no matter what way you twist and turn to avoid it. If so, the evil eye that Belinda placed on her husband Tom came to term when the five years was up. Tom knew his race was run, for he called Belinda in one evening when the prayers were said. He doused the candle by squeezing the burning wick to extinction with his thick fingers.

He said, 'I am going to have to leave you alone here, soon enough. You have been a faithful companion to me since we wed. For that reason I want you to take the money that I have kept beneath the bed and I want you to enjoy yourself while you live. Buy what you want with it, go wherever you like, but you must promise me one thing.'

She said, 'Of course, whatever you wish, for you have been a good husband to me in our time together and you have taught me many things.' But, what he said next shook her deeply, 'I will wait for you on the far side, no matter how long your time on earth should be. Since we married I have not been with another woman and I know that you have been faithful to me. So as a reward, we will be re-united forevermore in the next life.'

Belinda was a little nonplussed, as one might be at such a proposal, but she agreed for the moment, just in case he had any treasure stored away that she knew nothing about, as he had a great interest in the garden and was forever digging around at the back of the house. Then he said something else that unsettled her further, 'Take our candle and swear to me that so long as that candle shall burn, you will not allow your resolve to be swayed by any man.' This she did, for promising this was worth nothing, and Tom expired more or less the next day.

Neighbours came in and washed the dead man, shaved his stubble and placed his good wedding suit on him. His coffin was placed on their marital bed and a little table was placed at the end of the bed. Candlesticks were loaned by the priest and a saucer of holy water was left on the table near the open coffin where Tom lay sleeping his final sleep. Neighbours came in and commiserated with Belinda, then sprinkled holy water at the dead man while they said a silent prayer. Other neighbours made up sandwiches and they were placed on a large table in the back kitchen for visitors to help themselves. Tea was brewing all the time and there were bottles of drink for those that had a thirst on them.

It was at this point that Andrew wandered in to try his luck with the widow. He was a fine-looking chap that could have had his pick of the female population, but when he settled on nobody in particular, local interest waned in attracting him more permanently. This lack of interest on his part was a direct result of Andrew's fascination with the married Belinda. Standing beside her, he took her hand, in such a way that she was startled at his touch. 'I'm very sorry for your troubles', he whispered in a low voice. 'But I am touched by your quiet beauty and strength. And I wonder if I might call upon you in the days to come when the house is a bit quieter?' Belinda pulled her hand away from his, 'How dare you; can't you see I am in mourning for my late husband?'

'I can see that,' he replied. 'But your beauty of soul is such that I am touched by the thought of calling in and seeing you again. Alone.' He then stepped away from her. He threw a few drops of holy water in on the mortal remains of Tom in the coffin. They landed on his face and eyes. Tom wandered into the kitchen for some words with the local lads and a drop of whatever was going. Belinda moved from her place. She opened the high dark-wooded chest of drawers and took out the wedding candle. Other women watched with some interest as she placed the candle firmly on the table beside the coffin. 'It was Tom's favourite candle', she explained as she lit it with a taper from the lesser candles.

As the night drew on, men came from the kitchen and took up their places around the coffin. They were to stand watch through the long hours of night. It was what was done; no corpse lay alone in a Dublin household through the hours of darkness on the night before the funeral. Outside in the kitchen low songs were sung for the consolation and diversion of the living. Memories of the dead man were exchanged and stories were told to celebrate his time among them. A perfect balance between death and life was sought.

There was talk of the headless coachman and the black horses and the phantom coach coming along the road, and drinking continued. Andrew drank his share of a white liquid distilled locally in an informal way by an old neighbour of Tom's who was skilled in such matters. By the time he rose to leave, he had begun to sway gently. He would walk home, he announced, as he needed to sleep now to fortify himself against what was to come in the future. Nobody paid him much attention for people often speak nonsense in the early hours of the morning at a wake. He saluted all there and he saluted Belinda from the door of the coffin room and turned away.

What happened next became the stuff of legend and was re-told at other funerals. While Andrew left the house, intact and alive, he was found the following day lying face down on the road two parishes away. He had been hit by a passing truck with only one decent headlight working. He was carried along unbeknownst to the driver who did not know that he had hit Andrew in the dark. Neither was he aware that a body fell out from underneath the lorry as he crossed a hump-backed bridge some distance away. Ever afterwards, people at the wake swore they had heard horses hooves galloping past after Andrew left the house. They said he must have been taken into the coach, fought for his liberty and fallen out at the bridge.

In the bedroom, Belinda, who knew nothing of this, made sure Tom's candle burned down as swiftly as she could will it to. By dawn, it was guttering away and finally it sputtered out. As it went, she fancied she heard a noise from the bier. She looked at Tom's face. His face remained as it had been all night, but who knew what the dying candle light had shown as it finally expired.

14

LOST SHOES

Lack of footwear for children in poor parts of 1940s Dublin led to such a high level of school absenteeism that concerns were raised in the Dáil about the situation. An evening newspaper set up 'The Herald Boot Fund' to raise funds for the purchase of footwear for children in the city. Conferences of the St Vincent de Paul Society, the Children's Clothing Society, the Roomkeepers Society and the National Society for the Prevention of Cruelty to Children, all joined the effort to shoe the poor.

The problem was not unique to Dublin. Boots were issued by various local councils around the country to the deserving. Such footwear came with a council stamp placed resolutely on the sole of the boot, to prevent profiteering. This lead to major embarrassment, when the wearer knelt down in church and exposed his sole for all behind to see.

Hobnails placed underneath the boots made so much noise that when a troop of boys came along the busy streets of Dublin it was not unlike the sound a small invading army making its way along the thoroughfare. Add in the rattle of ball bearing wheels of numerous handcarts conveying everything from coal, to pig feed, to newspapers and fish for sale, and Dublin was a noisy place. Most families had a hand cart, or access to one, in an era when running a car or van was out of the question for most.

Imagine then the catastrophe facing a teenage Brian Byrne when he lost a new shoe in the river Liffey. The river's weirs were built to control the level of water on its journey to the sea. Included in their design were salmon chutes to aid spawning salmon on their annual journey upstream. To get to the grassy island, where it was safe to swim, local swimmers walked along the green mossy rounded tops of the weirs. Shoes had to be carried in the hand, trouser legs had to be rolled up, and a balancing act was employed to keep the wandering eye away from the rushing white water of the chute. It was heady stuff, right enough.

Brian, like all youngsters of the village, was used to the journey, but on this day, he was showing more bravado than wisdom. His mother told him not to go swimming and not to cross the weir so that no harm would come to his new shoes, bought at enormous sacrifice by his mother ahead of his return to schooling come the autumn. On this day, he wore them to allow the leather to find its way around the outline of his feet; to break them in, was another way of putting it.

Brian headed straight to the river for a swim in his skimpys with the other lads. He knew he could dry off by borrowing the damp towels of the others when they were finished with them. No one need know he had been swimming at all. The group of boys stood together on the bank before the crossing was ventured. They silently observed the quiet flow of the river. Each pulled off their cheap rubber plimsolls and started off, one after the other.

Brian had knotted the laces of his expensive shoes together and wore them tied around his neck. That way, everyone could see how well-to-do he was and they could see how little it fazed him that he had to be careful of his charges. Inevitably, however, the laces came undone. The shoes fell away from their berth around his neck, one towards the deep water, the other towards the rushing white cascade. It bobbed resolutely down the wall of the weir to the level below. Brian caught the shoe heading for the depths, but he should have caught the other one first. The shoe at the bottom of the deep water could have been dived for, and would have provided a warm afternoon's sport for the excited youngsters. By the time Brian had caught one falling shoe and regained his balance on the slippery weir surface, the other shoe had begun a journey of its own into the unknown. It was never seen again and simply passed into a history of boyhood.

It presented a very real problem for all concerned, not least Brian who was now the possessor of a single leather shoe, when quite recently he had sported a fine pair of shoes. That the shoe was lost was bad enough. The pair was broken, never to be reconciled again. That his mother was going to be as wild as a river in flood was also a given; but the certainty that his avenging father would hear about it loomed larger in all of their minds as it was accepted that the loss of the shoe was a problem for the community of boys and not just for Brian Byrne. They held a conference on the bank of the river with their feet dangling in the cool water.

It was soon confirmed that the shoes were purchased by means of a cheque from the cheque man. This was a glorified method of money lending whereby a client was given a cheque to be spent in a range of approved establishments. The recipient then paid back the amount plus interest to a collector, each week, who called to homes on a regular round of payment gathering. The particular shop that had supplied

Brian's new shoes was quickly established by dint of collective knowledge.

The group went there in their summer footwear, many with toes peeking through the cheap material. They halted a distance away from the shop and held a council of war. The little shop was wedged in a small space along a busy Thomas Street. An intoxicatingly strong smell of leather and dyes pervaded the shop. The premises was so old that its dark corners were lit by gas light. The shoemaker was a cordial character, but contrary at times when lounging visitors impeded his work. At such times he was less tactful. Bowing to economic reality and changes in demand, he allowed his son to begin to stock and sell ready-made shoes in the front part of the shop. He thought little of the new staples and glue-line shoes that his customers wanted to try on, rather than wait for a decent pair to be fashioned for them. But that was progress.

His son was away when Brian Byrne stood at the counter with a single new shoe. On his feet were borrowed plimsolls. Their owner sat up the street with his feet drawn up beneath him so no one would notice his feet were now bare. Brian placed the single shoe on the counter and waited for the shoemaker to ask him what he wanted. 'My mother said can I have the other shoe,' he said with all the conviction of a condemned man arguing his innocence.

'What other shoe?'

'She wanted to buy these shoes for me yesterday for school. So she brought this one home to see if it would fit me. It does, so she says she'll take the pair. She left the cheque yesterday, she told me to tell you.' The shoemaker told Brian to go home or he'd tell his mother on him. Brian replied that his mother had a brother home from the merchant navy and she would send him in to get the pair of shoes that was paid for by cheque. The brother was a deaf mute and there was no talking to him when he was angry, Brian added. And the cheque man would have to hear about it as well and he would probably be cross when he heard what had happened to his good cheque. The shoemaker offered to give Brian a clout about the ears if he didn't get out, but such was the passion Brian brought to his perform-ance that the shoemaker began to wonder if his son had actually stocked the shoes and had given one out to see if it would fit the boy.

By now, the argument had given courage to the other boys who gathered around the shop to lend support. They did this by pretending they did not know Brian at all and they were interested and fair observers of all that went on. The shoemaker responded by offering to let the dogs out to eat them. He had no dogs, but the threat made the boys qui-eten down and move away from the door. That only made room for passing adults to peer in at the goings-on, for eve-ryone in Dublin loves a good argument. In the heel of the hunt, the shoemaker could get nothing else done until he resolved the issue. 'Give me the shoe', he demanded. 'What is your mother's name and address, so I can tell the cheque man to check up on this?' Personal ID was unheard of at this time so it was easy for Brian to give a completely bogus name and address.

Quite naturally, the shoemaker could not find the miss-ing shoe in the shop. He looked at Brian and at his feet and, with the acute knowledge of the true shoemaker, knew the exact size that would fit the boy before him. He pulled out a pair of shoes that were somewhat of the same colour and design as the cheap shoe before him. He handed them over to Brian with a gruff order to try them on before he left the shop.

'Both of them, and give those old runners back to that young lad sitting on his own up the street while all your gang is down here telling lies.' An astonished Brian dis-covered that the shoes fitted him perfectly and that the shoemaker was not going to give him back the only shoe of the previous pair. He kept that he said for reference. Maybe a one legged boy will make use of it he said, as Brian and the gang took themselves off towards distant home.

His mother was astonished when he returned home wearing a different pair of shoes to the ones he had left home in that morning. By now an accomplished liar, Brian patiently explained that the other pair had been pinching him. So, he went back to the shoe shop and swopped them for a more comfortable pair. Was that alright? Faced with this *fait accompli* and not wishing to probe too far into the lie, she said it was. His father, for his part, was well pleased with his son's resolution of the issue for he had lost a good few shoes himself on that weir when he was a young man: so he said no more; sometimes it is better to let life flow on gently wherever it will, and to remain quiet, for the sake of wisdom.

BANG BANG

Dublin would be nothing without its characters. One of the characters that cast the longest shadow across the streets of his native city was a simple man who shot dead as many people as he could manage in a day's ride across the metropolis. Not only did he shoot some unsuspecting passers-by, but countless Dubliners began to return fire when Bang Bang Thomas Dudley opened up fire on them.

Such spontaneous gun battles would startle visitors to Dublin who were unaware that as non-combatants they were perfectly safe. It was not unusual to see large numbers of people firing imaginary guns at a poorly dressed man who was hanging from the safety pole on the open platform on the back of a city bus. For Bang Bang would open hostilities by pointing a large key at you and shouting, 'Bang, bang. You're dead', in such a way that you felt you had to react in some meaningful way. It was an invitation to play a game that few could resist.

The imaginary bullets rendered you either dead or 'roonded', this being Dublinese for 'wounded'. But even if you opted for death, either an instant release and fall against a wall or an adjacent shop window or a long lingering stagger about the place, you could still get back in the game by counting from one to ten, slowly, and you were ready to go again. You were either ready to continue your daily duties, as if nothing had happened, or, if the bus had not moved too far away, you could rejoin the battle. It was a little different for the shoals of cyclists who inhabited the streets of Dublin in the 1940s and '50s when Bang Bang was at the height of his marauding campaign. A cyclist shot at by Bang Bang was free to duck the bullet and to return fire from the bicycle now transformed into the steed of an outlaw or the unsaddled mount of a red Indian, bent on scalping the entire bus load of happy passengers. Add the pursuing cyclists to the staggering pedestrians breathing their last on the mean streets of Dublin town and you can see how one man with the mind of a child brightened the day for many Dubliners.

The 1940s and '50s, when Bang Bang rode across the prairie of his mind, was the era of the Hollywood western. In a time before television brought images and sound to people's homes, the main entertainment was cinema. Every parish had its local cinema, and it seemed for a while as if every street in Dublin city sported a picture palace. The Corinthian Cinema on Eden Quay, just yards from O'Connell Street, was known as 'The Ranch' for its consistent programming of double-bill westerns. So popular were the pictures that queues formed outside cinemas. Ticket buyers often came in midway through a film, watched the story to the end, and then sat through the next showing until 'where I came in' came along and they left again. To a populace used to this way of story watching, and assembling the complete narrative in their heads on the way home afterwards, a man on a bus firing shots from a four-inch brass key came as little surprise

Bang Bang's gun was an ornate key that now sits in the city archives on Pearse Street in a glass case on a red cushion for all to see. It may not be the original key; Bang Bang told a radio interviewer many years earlier that he lost the key he had used for forty years on Meath Street before replacing it with another key. It is a key that brought a city to its knees with laughter and enjoyment. It was the key to a city's imagination. Bang Bang often claimed that he and that other great shooter of a gun John Wayne were born in the same year. However, Wayne was born in 1907 which made Bang Bang his elder by a year. Wayne should have taken cowboy tips from his elder.

People were sometimes startled when they would be minding their own business and a hitherto silent Bang Bang opened fire and in a loud voice told them that they were dead because they had let their guard slip as they moseyed along. Once the bus halted at a stop for disgorging or loading passengers, Bang Bang would step off the platform to allow the conductor do his job in marshalling the passengers to their seats before hitting the bell twice to tell the driver to drive on. One bell was to stop, two to go, three for emergency stop. Nothing could be simpler. Still, on some occasions the bus would pull away without the armed guard and he would have to sprint after it to hop aboard the back platform on the way to his next episode. On the occasions when he fell off the bus without quite meaning to do so, he would call out that he was alright and that the driver should keep the stagecoach going to the next town; he would catch up. He would then gallop up the street slapping his backside as if he was whipping a horse along beneath his spurs.

Traffic on most of the city junctions in those years was controlled by gardaí on point duty who used white batons to direct traffic movements. It was a particular joy for Bang Bang to engage a jaded point man in a discreet shooting match between a Garda traffic baton and a large brass key. The lawman always won. Occasionally one might pretend that he was slightly wounded by Bang Bang's expert marksmanship, but this was only as a salute to a worthy opponent. Bang Bang was nothing if not precise about the parameters of the game. The good guys always prevailed, as they did in the movies.

Bang Bang's name was Thomas Dudley, the son of Mary and John Dudley. He was born on 12 February 1906.

Thomas was to want for close family love most of his life. His father and siblings all died when Thomas was very young, as was the way with many impoverished families. He was sent to an orphanage in Cabra in the North of Dublin when his mother was unable to support him. His mother died in 1933, when Thomas was twenty-seven years old. Thomas Dudley lived his adult life in the Liberties area on the southside when he wasn't roaming Dublin guarding make-believe stagecoaches from renegades, and keeping the place safe for law-abiding citizens.

He lived on Mill Lane for more than forty years and later lived in Bridgefoot Street flats near the city quays. He suffered from bad eyesight and when his vision was almost completely gone he was housed in Clonturk House for the Adult Blind in Drumcondra, once more on the north side of Dublin. There he received visitors. He told those that would listen that he wished now to be known as Lord Dudley. Still using a title and a nick-name Thomas Dudley passed away on 12 January 1981.

His passing was noted by all and sundry, the high and the mighty and his partners across the prairie of his mind. His death at seventy-five years of age even drew obituaries in the national newspapers, of which he would have been quite proud. He was buried in a clerical grave-yard a few hundred metres away from the home he had known in his declining years.

Bang Bang lived his time when Dublin was still more of a large town than the sprawling city it became. It was common to be given a nickname in Dublin and once given, the name stuck with you for life. Thomas Dudley would tell people that his name was Thomas Dudley, Thomas Dudley, D, U, D, L, E, Y, as if he wanted to be sure that people knew he was more than his nickname.

To celebrate his life and to mark the thirtieth anniversary of his death, *The Mooney Show* on RTÉ carried a feature dedicated to the Dubliner, during which his shooting key was presented to the Lord Mayor, Councillor Gerry Breen. The Lord Mayor passed in on to Dublin City Library and Archive on Pearse Street where Bang Bang's key takes pride of place inside a glass display case.

Whether it's still loaded or not is anyone's guess.

Just be ready to duck when you approach the imaginary gun, for there is no telling whether or not the ghost of Bang Bang still rides the streets of Dublin. He might just ask you to join in a game of cowboys of the mind.

16

ROBBING THE GUESTS

A man once came to the city of Dublin thinking the world to be a wonderful place and the city of Dublin to be sophistication itself. He was a dreamer and a seller of goods. He knew the people of Dublin would buy sufficient merchandise from him so that he would become wealthy and would be able to buy a house in Dublin or at least in one of the villages on its outskirts.

He rode a horse that was neither a new horse nor an old horse, but a horse that was good enough for the job. The horse was not a pack-animal. It carried just one person, himself, in comfort. For the carrying of goods for sale he had an ass, whose rein he tied to the saddle of his horse and so they moved along like a small caravan.

He wore a soft hat and leggings, and sported a fine black moustache that matched his black coat. He always had a jest and a laugh with his customers, as all good merchants do. His twin-animal caravan was unusual for the Dublin of olden times, for most goods transported by horse sat on a wheeled cart of some kind or other, the better to transport them through the city without tiring the draught animal. All goods essential to daily living were delivered by horse-drawn means in the city. Coal, milk, bread and all the necessities of life began and ended their journeys around the city by horse.

Dublin did not stretch much past the surrounding canals or past Islandbridge to the west. Everything was within a comfortable range for an Irish draught horse going about its business. The man found the size of the city to be comfortable for his purposes. He sold a little in the markets and he sold a little by standing on the streets offering his goods to passers-by who had not been to the market. Whatever was left over, he sold door-to-door at a reduced price so he might empty the packs on his ass who by now was tired of carrying things.

Most nights, the man passed the hours of darkness in Dublin, resuming his homeward journey on the following day. He chose accommodation that was close to the western outskirts of Dublin for his base and home was west to the midlands. He changed accommodation each time he stayed in Dublin lest footpads be watching him and rob him of his day's takings.

One night, he went to some lodgings he had been told about near Bridgefoot Street. He was told there were stables in the back and a gate that locked to keep the animals safe and sound through the night. The landlady showed him to a small room at the top of the old building. He shared this with three other men. They all snored in their sleep. Afterwards, he blamed the noise from their snoring for his inattention to the security of his animals. He was a light sleeper, but had slept deeply when he did nod off from exhaustion in the early hours of the morning.

When he arose, he went to feed his animals. He found two animals in the stable, the same number that he had left there. The ass, however, was not the one he had said goodnight to the night before. In its stead was an animal of the same race, but one that would not pass the bridge of Islandbridge a half mile away without being carried by someone else. Its young days were gone as were its older days, almost. It was a morose ass who was fed up with life.

The landlady said the gates had been locked through the night. She showed the man that they were still secured.

It was dark when he had come in with the ass. Was he sure it was his that he had brought in last night? Did someone switch it on him while he was inside someone else's house delivering the last of his goods? How tired had he been when he came in to sleep? Maybe even now someone else had an ass that was not his either. If he took the two animals that were there now and walked along the city quays for the morning, perhaps the owner of the ass he now possessed would make himself known to the man.

She went on like this until the man grew weary of her talk. His only opportunity of finding it was to take to the streets and to ask passers-by if they had seen it anywhere. But in a city filled with four-legged beasts of burden, it proved impossible to locate his stolen ass. He gave up eventually and gave the reins of the weak animal to a beggar man to take to the knackers yard, where he might receive a few pence for the carcass.

He headed for home on his horse at a faster clip than normal, for he wanted to be away from the scene of his misfortune as swiftly as possible. It was to be some time before he gathered together a new consignment of goods for sale in Dublin. He brought a new ass with him this time.

That night he returned to the lodging house near Bridgefoot Street and once more stabled his animals behind a locked street gate. On his way in, he witnessed a young man dressed in poor clothes being roughly evicted from the premises for claiming that he had been robbed while he slept the night before. His frame was skinny and he wore burst boots on his stockingless feet.

The man waited until the burly guardians stepped back inside and closed the door behind them with a bang. He asked the younger man to tell him what had happened. He was not surprised to hear that he had been asked to sleep where three snoring men slept and that he had fallen asleep with exhaustion after hours of unrest. When he awoke his purse was gone. His good leather boots were replaced by the old scrags of things he now wore on his feet. The landlady told him she had seen some young boys running away and that he should follow to see where they went. Most likely they had taken the purse, and his boots by mistake.

He learnt that the young man's savings had been in the wallet. They spoke some more and they struck a bargain. The younger man would keep watch on the man's animals through the night. When morning came, the man would see that he received full restitution for his loss.

When he entered the premises to greet the landlady, she was attentive in her responses to his questions on the availability of a bed for the night and a secure livery stable for his animals. He guessed correctly that she never forgot the faces of her guests, particularly one who had suffered a loss on her premises. They agreed on a price for a room where he would sleep alone. He inspected the room, expressed satisfaction, and fell into conversation with the landlady about the safety of cash and goods on the premises, in these dangerous times.

She was cautious in her responses, but more than a little interested in his conversation about cheques made out to the bearer to be paid from the account holder's bank. Cheques were not commonplace in those times and the landlady was an easy subject for what happened next, for it is said that it is easy enough to rob a robber.

He told her that he had made a lot of cash that day as he had sold all that he had brought with him to the city. He had met a man from Liverpool at an eating place and they had made a commercial agreement to do with the Liverpudlian returning to that city and shipping goods to Dublin in return for the cash he had just now received from the man. What had that to with her, wondered the landlady. The man told her that there would be increased traffic between the two ports and most of the Liverpudlian visitors would need accommodation; he hoped that the landlady would be able to offer them lodgings. He recalled her assistance in the matter of the missing ass and it was this more than anything else that had caused him to recommend her to others. The landlady's cupidity made her lessen her defences, despite her initial reticence. The man then proposed a business proposition between the two of them. He was by now entirely without any money to pay her for her lodgings, or to buy a second ass on his way home on the morrow, a beast he would need to take care of the increased business that was sure to be quite close to realisation.

'What has this to with me?' she asked warily. It's a cash establishment. You pay or you leave, now. The man agreed that this was an excellent way to do business. One he adhered to himself. But he had a solution: with the good lady's agreement, he would write out a cheque for £100 and present it to the landlady in exchange for just £90 from her cash tin. She would show an immediate profit and he would have cash with which to pay her for his board for the night. If the landlady was a cute thief she was not a clever business person. Greed overcame her caution. She paid over £90 in notes and coins and waited while the man wrote her name on the cheque in copperplate with ink from a fountain pen and filled in £100 as the amount to be released to the holder on presentation to his bank.

Next morning, he paid over the cost of the night's lodging for one person and two animals in cash. He thanked the landlady and reminded her, who had no need of reminding, that the longer she held onto the cheque the more valuable it would become as profits in bank shares rose. As they rose, so did the value of all cheques held out for encashment, he assured her. The man rode off then with his horse and ass safe, well and rested. On the way, he met the young man and paid him every penny he had lost in the boarding house.

In the boarding house, the landlady placed the cheque behind a mirror in the best parlour where sat the piano and where no one was allowed to sleep. Time passed and one month followed another in such an orderly manner that years followed on behind them, as was to be expected. The man grew older and his sons took over the business and one fine morning in the month of June they discovered their father had passed away in his sleep.

The landlady too grew older and one day decided she should cash the cheque with its accumulated profits. The bank manger refused payment on the cheque. He told the landlady that, not only was there no such thing as accumulated profits on a cheque, but that the pay-by date had passed many years before so the cheque was invalid, in any case. Further, he told the astonished thief of a landlady, the cheque was issued on an account that had lasted just one day and there had never been any more than £5 in funds in the account. Also, no one in the bank had ever heard of a Patrick Asal in whose name the account was opened and closed in. The landlady went home and smashed the mirror but not before she had turned the cheque over and had read on the back a note that said the word *Asal* was simply the word for ass. And the issuer wished her well on her journey through life on her stolen ass.

17

WIGS AWAY

In Dublin, long ago, people used combs to rid their itching hair of nits. When they finished with the combs, they threw them away. Many centuries later, the broken combs were dug up and discussed by learned people seeking clues as to how other people lived their lives in a different time. Various assumptions were made about the life and daily customs of a people who did not have access to showers, bathrooms or Jacuzzis to help maintain a high standard of personal hygiene. Few homes had a piped water supply and most relied on a communal standpipe or rainwater gathered in tubs. Personal bathing may not have been as regular as modern citizens now expect.

Mostly, Dubliners wanted to stop their hair itching, one supposes, and when the comb's teeth no longer did that well, they threw it away and began afresh with a new comb. A nit-free life apart, hair is important to most people. Those who have it and those who do not have it alike.

Since our hair is often the first thing many people see of us, some people take extraordinary care that their hair and its styling is appropriate to the occasion. In genteel society in Dublin and after the restoration of the monarchy under Charles II – following the disastrous hair days of Oliver Cromwell – wigs were worn over the person's natural hair.

While wigs were and are worn for style purposes, medical reasons, and to hide hair loss, wigs worn in Restoration Ireland resembled nothing more than a small sheepskin sitting on the head of the wearer. They covered the head entirely. Tresses fell fetchingly down the cheeks of wearers and the rest flowed around the shoulders and back of the wearer.

A wig used to be called a periwig and was then shortened to wig. They were made of horse hair, or the hair from humans who no longer needed it, either because it was too long and needed to be shorn, or they were dead and had no use for it anymore. This use of a dead person's hair could have consequences for the wearer. The deceased might have passed on their head lice to their successor or they could have died of disease and the infection might linger in the wig.

A plague in the 1660s in London resulted in a reluctance among wig wearers to wear their new wigs lest their provenance proved to be that of a plague victim. The unhygienic conditions of the time meant that hair attracted head lice, which quite simply hopped from one head of hair to another, without any intimacy being involved at all by the host heads. It was a problem that could be reduced if natural hair was shaved and replaced with a wig that could be more easily de-loused. As practical life trundled along, wigs became smaller and sat instead on the scalp of the wearer. Many were off-white and powdered, and were obviously not the genuine hair of the person before you. Nor were they supposed to be. Nonetheless, since people like to change their appearance from time to time, dyeing of hair became popular.

A story is told that in the dying years of the nineteenth century, Isaac Butt, a founder of the Home Rule Movement, liked to tint his hair a different colour than the one nature blessed him with. He asked an employee to help out with a pair of bottles the hairdresser had left with him, for such an occasion. A mistake in mixing the content resulted in Butt appearing with green hair, hardly an inappropriate colour, but not exactly what had been envisaged, by Butt or his hairdresser. This was neither the first nor the last time that a hairdresser was involved in a strange hair story.

While Butt was a nationalist and a busy lawyer, he lived life to the full and spent money as freely as he earned it. He was also reputed to be a man who loved women too often and too much. At one time, he found himself lodged in the Debtors' Prison on Thomas Street for non-payment of his due bills. He was transferred to Kilmainham Jail and eventually managed to find a way to be released. Many many years later, another man came to grief over a head of hair on High Street, not far from where Butt had languished in imprisonment.

Simon and Michael were friends who had been to college together. Simon dropped out to live the life of a rover and to travel the road to self realisation. Simon vanished somewhere around India. He was last seen boarding the Magic Bus in Dublin with a backpack and his hair draped around his shoulders in memory of Restoration Dublin and as a salute to the new world he was to inhabit. For a while, he posted postcards of where he was to open the eyes of those left behind to the possibilities of the world. Then they stopped. Michael stayed on to the end of his studies and became a successful businessman. He joined the family shipping agency and soon took over the company. Years passed. Michael grew stouter and wealthier. Simon was nowhere to be seen.

Michael's family grew up and left his home. His wife grew fatter and lazier and complained all day long. His business was so prosperous that he hired workers to do the work he used to do himself. So, when a young woman put her eyes on his wealth he was pleased with her attentions. Of course, she did not say she lusted for his riches. He believed her when she said she absolutely respected his life arrangement with his wife and family, and would not care if he was rich or poor. She liked his companionship and she liked to hear how he bested the vicissitudes of life to get to where he was now. She said he was entitled to some fun in life. Her name was Tanya and she wanted nothing of him except companionship. And that is when Simon came home from his travels.

Michael was sitting in a bar on High Street awaiting Tanya's arrival. Tanya was never less than ten minutes late for any date they had. She liked to keep Michael waiting for her. However, that ten minutes was her downfall on this fine June evening, for Michael wandered out onto the street to take the air. Simon, who had just returned from his travels, caught his old friend by the elbow and said it was high time they painted the town red. A startled but delighted Michael soon found himself immersed in the night life of Temple Bar as Simon swept him along in their recalled exuberance.

Tanya was abandoned, as the pals wandered from pub to pub up and down every narrow street of the old town. Simon challenged Michael to name the street before they entered it. The loser paid for the next drink. After a while, they could neither remember where they were or what anything was called any more. Simon still wore loose, flowing clothes and still wore his hair long although now it was tied in a ponytail so that it wouldn't get into his drink.

The conversation moved to Michael's neat back-and-sides hairstyle. He said he liked it like that. Simon said it was time he stood out from the ordinary and re-claimed his youthful zest for life. In short, he needed a new hairstyle.

Many a decision made early in the morning, in the company of like-minded souls can come to be regretted. To wit: Simon now revealed himself as the owner of a chain of men's barbers across Europe. He started his business in Vienna years earlier, when he had grown weary of the road and wanted to settle. The chain was known as 'Simple Simon's Really Nice Barbers. They'd cut the hairs of heads of state, according to Simon. They'd cut the hair of semi-bald men requiring just the short sides to be trimmed. In fact, movie stars and celebrities of all sorts were secret customers of Simon's flying scissors. He was in Dublin he revealed, to open a nationwide chain of 'Simple Simon's'.

As it happened, there were premises nearby to which he had the keys and on which he was about to sign the lease. He suggested going there and they would re-style Michael into the man he always was. Michael agreed it was an excellent idea. They went to the premises and Michael blinked as a row of blinding lights came on in predictable succession. 'Take a chair', said Simon grandly. 'This is the first day of the rest of your life.'

Michael wondered if now would be a good time to tell the companion of his younger years that he was completely bald beneath his very expensive hairpiece. The barber chose the chair in the window that passers-by could see. Michael became worried about being embarrassed in full view of the passing populace of Dublin. But he need not have worried, for an eagle-eyed Simon had already spotted the wig. A good barber was a man of immense discretion. A necessary characteristic for one privy to such confidences as which way a man parted his hair and, for that matter, which hair was the man's own and which hair was imported, either from a horse or someone else's head.

Simon said it would be best if he used a new Viennese method of trimming a man's hair without having to wash it. So Michael got comfortable in his chair and became so relaxed that he fell asleep with the mesmeric clicking of a hand scissors and the swirling comfort of a bellyful of intoxicating liquor. Simon became so absorbed in his work that he removed the hair piece altogether and brought it to a brighter light deeper in the shop to work upon it while his friend slept the sleep of the just.

There were a number of spare wigs there awaiting collection by their owners for one reason or another. Simon placed his friend's hair piece beside one that was dyed green for a stage comedian's next show. He quite forgot about it when he turned and saw Michael hiding behind the chair. There was a face at the window, staring in. It was Tanya, furious that she had been left behind by Michael. She had spotted him in the chair and was banging the window, shouting something or other that was probably inappropriate for a girl friend to be shouting at a married man. She was having a bad hair night, for sure. Michael was hiding from her, for he had seen his present state in the huge mirror in front of his chair. His baldness was there for all to see. He did not wish to be uncovered by this young woman with the wicked tongue. Simon, ever the soul of discretion, hurried back and caught up the wig for Michael to don as quickly as possible. Michael grabbed the hairpiece, stuck it on top of his head and opened the door to the street. An astonished Tanya stopped complaining in her shock at the green-haired man before her. For Simon had picked up the comedian's novelty hairpiece in error in his haste.

Michael, sporting his green hair, trotted after her into the night, for there was no knowing what she would do. Simon watched them and sighed for the days of the Magic Bus and the gentle lunatics with long hair that travelled on it. At least he knew that the journey was going to end. Dublin had grown too hectic for him while he was away and he longed to be somewhere else.

18

HONEYMOONS

When a newly-married couple told their Dublin wedding guests that they were touring Ireland for their honeymoon, it meant they were going to an auntie down the country for a week or less, depending on funds and the auntie. Income levels were not so high, at the time, so that couples couldn't fly off to the southern hemisphere on their first married holiday together.

Weddings had to be planned and guest lists agreed. Mortal enemies had to be seated away from one another. That is, if the reception was to be in a hotel or a marquee in the back garden or something posh like that. Mostly, it was a hooley in the kitchen of the bride's family home. The bride's family paid for the reception by and large, as best they could. Everyone had to save up for it from their weekly wage. A wedding cake was bought, as was porter and stout and beer and perhaps a few bottles of whisky, to cut the phlegm for the volunteer singers before they launched into their well-rehearsed party pieces. There would be a few bottles of sweet sherry for those that declared themselves to be non-drinkers. Once the food was gone and the drinking commenced, a space was cleared for dancing, and whoever had an instrument and knew how to play would start the music. And so the evening would progress.

When it came time for the happy couple to depart, the tradition was to mess up the groom as much as possible and to leave him dishevelled and disoriented. It was a big day in anyone's life, especially in a country with no divorce. The first week was often the biggest trial for a new couple. If they survived seven days of one another's unremitting company they were over the first hurdle. For if they did not go away on a honeymoon there were customs to be adhered to.

Newlyweds who could not afford to honeymoon somewhere else were supposed to stay indoors for a week. Perhaps in the hope that people would think they were away somewhere if they were not seen in their usual haunts. Custom dictated that a sharp knife was not to be used in preparation of food for that week. This might result in near starvation and a severe trying of matrimonial bonds if the two people did not meet one another half way.

Certainly one couple were observed attacking one another with hatchets on Gloucester Street outside their new home on the morning after their wedding reception. It caused quite a stir, for they had been dancing to waltz music on a melodeon played by Christy McGrane until the small hours. They were disarmed eventually, and the families concerned began to negotiate and propose possible solutions. No one knew what had caused the falling out. After all, they had saved money well; even walking home from the picture house to save the bus fare in the weeks before the nuptials. They managed to save £119 in the run-up to the off. They bought a bedroom suite, a dining-room suite, a kitchen dresser and two chairs. The flat already had a gas cooker in it with three rings that worked. The bride's mother gave them a pair of curtains for the window and all was set fair. Until the hatchets came out.

What perplexed a good few people was the presence of two hatchets in a new household. Most agreed that there had probably been a double up in the wedding presents list, though a few bags of coal would probably have served the new family better than a pair of China-made hatchets with blades that would go blunt very easily.

Someone said the ill feeling started when Ned carried Olive across the threshold with more enthusiasm than accuracy. It was believed that if a wife stumbled over the threshold, then bad luck would come to her marriage. How much worse was it when she entrusted herself to her new husband and he fell over the threshold and let the two of them fall down on top of the presents. When a confused Olive arose, it was to find that one of the three ducks that were to be hung on the wall was now wingless. There were only two ducks left worth talking about. She pointed this out to her new husband Ned, who said he did not care who gave the gift to them: two ducks were as good as three and twice as good as one. One word let to another until they spilled out onto the street the following morning, intent on an immediate separation of the other from the planet. Matters calmed down after a new set of ducks was produced by a woman on the husband's side and they agreed to give their marriage another try.

These were the days when marriages were either arranged, or took place among people from the same community, which was much the same thing for if an unsuitable match was in the offing, wagging tongues would point out the unsuitability of the pairing. Few courtships survived a disapproving parish.

Consider then the case of the woman who met a man on the internet. When they met in real life, they fell in love straight away and agreed they would be married before a year had passed. They were both from Dublin, but hailed from the suburbs at opposite ends of the city. So large had Dublin become that the old bonds of community were weakened and neither knew the other's background as well as they might.

The man was rich but did not tell Lara this for he wanted to test her love for him first. She told him, often as she could that she considered happiness and love to be wealth, not possessions. But Steve doubted her love and told her a lie to see how she would respond. His parents had left the bulk of his inheritance to him in gold coins that lay behind a hidden door in the cellar beneath his old inherited house. One day, he told Lara he owned a single gold coin. He said it was hidden in the depth of the garden for fear his house would be robbed. He brought her to the place in the garden to show her. He made her swear to tell nobody their secret, which she did to humour him, though she thought him even more loveable for asking such a thing. Then, he wrapped a piece of lead, the size of a large coin, in a cloth and buried it there when he was alone. Each day the girl visited, Steve watched to see that the ground was undisturbed. Each day, the girl smiled and told him she would love him even if he penniless. Still he watched his garden.

Time passed and the ground remained as it was. He became ashamed of himself. He removed the lead and its cloth covering and smoothed the ground. But when he went to visit his gold coins in the cellar of his home he found they were gone. He found a note in Lara's handwriting saying the following, 'If you value gold more than love, then you had best spend your days with your true love.' There was no gold to be found anywhere in the cellar. He thought that he had been right all along: she was a gold digger.

Lara had disappeared, her account on the internet where they had first met was closed and her telephone number was discontinued. When he drove to where she lived, her apartment was to let. It was empty and no one could tell him where she had gone. The value of the gold coins was such that the Garda would begin an immediate investigation if they were informed. Nevertheless, he hesitated to explain to someone else how he had tempted his future wife to steal from him and how she had yielded to that temptation.

He was a man with a steady profession and an assured income so he did not want for anything in a material way.

Each night, he logged on to the internet and searched for her name to see if she was to be found elsewhere. He used many variants of her name, but to no avail.

It is true that when you do not have something it seems you will see it all about you. Without a fiancé, it seemed to Steve that on every road he travelled there was a chapel or church or meeting house where a couple was being married to the great joy of the assembled wedding guests. Each time Steve saw a bride floating along in a white dress, he returned home to search his house once more for a clue to the disappearance of his fortune and his fiancé.

One day, he pushed open the door to the bedroom Lara used to sleep in when she stayed with him, for he had insisted they sleep apart until their wedding night. He leaned against the frame and looked around the room that used to be his nursery when he was little. It was a place he did not like to enter as it had been the private place of his fiancé. For no reason that he could fathom, Steve found himself drawn to the neat little bed. He sat down on it to be closer to Lara's absent presence. He became aware of something underneath the bed clothes which was making him uncomfortable. When he turned over the bed clothes he found every single coin of gold that he owned, together with a single faded rose from his garden.

19

TELEVISION THIEVES

Four young men decided that it was easier to be thieves than to work and so they launched into a life of crime. They robbed and stole whenever opportunity presented itself, but they made a fatal mistake in what was to be their biggest robbery.

In the early 1960s, they were charmed like everyone else in Dublin with the arrival of the new national television station. They were particularly interested in the crime drama. One crucial fact eluded them and that was that in all of these programmes the bad guys lost and the good guys won. Basic morality was not their strong suit, and so they missed the point. They fancied the criminal life and given their lack of knowledge of fine art or jewels, they settled for robbing small shops and unsuspecting householders who had left their homes unlocked.

In the 1960s, few people could afford television sets when the new national service began broadcasting. To meet a market need, astute traders made sets available through a weekly rental plan. To ensure payments were kept up to date they employed door-to-door collectors to gather in the weekly amount. In return, the hiree had immediate access to television and world television programming for a small weekly payment. Should anything go wrong, as it frequently did with the early models, the set would be serviced by the renter. The hire collector became a familiar guest in those households that were willing to pay him as agreed. Other householders refused to answer the door when he called, as they had no money to pay for the week and had no intention of surrendering the rental set either.

At this time in Ireland there was a very relaxed attitude to the procreation of dogs. The pups were of many strands of lineage and were designated as mongrels. Nearly every household had a dog which would be allowed to roam the streets at will. When a bitch came into heat, every male dog for miles around would stand guard outside her house for a chance to say hello, should she be allowed out by her unthinking owner. This led to many litters of pups being born. Few people had the heart to kill the pups so homes were normally found for them. This meant that most homes had a dog in residence, which might or might not bite the collector upon their arrival, depending on the disposition of the animal on the day. This fact was to play a crucial part in the investigation of the gang's final act of robbing Noel, the collector, of his collected rentals. They'd decided that this would be best done on a Friday night, on a quiet street, when Noel had called to his last house. He would be relaxed at that point, they reasoned, and a little less on his guard than at other times.

However, Noel was not the premier television rental collector for nothing. He frequently changed routes and times and was as often as not to be found concluding his run where he should have been starting from. In frustration, the four thieves, Andy, Derek, Barry and Brian, robbed anyone they met when Noel did not show up. It was reported in the local papers as a crime spree. They were masked and could appear anywhere at any time, an excited reporter stated. In fact, the masked robbers, on one occasion, struck in two different places at the same time, a worrying development for the local forces of law and order. This was because they had spilt up to increase their chances of accosting Noel.

As it happened, on this night, Noel had accepted the offer of tea and homemade scones from a recently widowed client. She said she was considering getting a bigger television set for her home, now that the insurance money on her dead husband had arrived. She asked Noel to sit down with her for a while, which he did. There he stayed until it was so late in the night that the milkman had begun his delivery to the sleeping houses all around where the widow lived. Once more, Andy, Derek, Barry and Brian were left short of Noel's collection. Once more, they were vexed. They began to believe that Noel knew they planned to rob him. Andy, the oldest of the four and unofficial leader, believed that he was playing cat and mouse with them. His followers, Derek, Barry and Brian, hardly had one collective brain of a single robber between them.

Despite this, they conspired to set a trap for Noel one dark night. They each posted themselves in a different place to watch for the arrival of the collector. They each stood beside a public phone box so they could ring Derek, the liaison man, when they saw where Noel was beginning his round. As communications officer, Derek was to be rung once and told the agreed codeword of 'Christmas', to show they were in situ. Soon enough, the phone rang. It was Barry who said 'Christmas has come early to his part of the world.' Which was the complicated code for 'Noel is here'. Derek rang Andy and Brian to alert them that the operation was on. The caper had begun.

Brian's location was where they believed Noel's journey would conclude. He brought his mongrel Jack-Russell-looking dog along with him to deal with any other dogs that might cause them difficulties. They would need to concentrate when the action started and they could not have stray dogs attacking them or barking or anything like that. Their plan was going well; each reported to Derek on Noel's progress as he neared the end of the houses where Brian and his dog waited in expectation. Brian watched as Noel entered the final house. He waved to the others to gather around him and his dog for the culmination of the plan. They dug deep in their jacket pockets. Each produced a balaclava hood that left only the eyes and mouths exposed. They each donned a boiler suit bought a few days previously.

They were now masked and suited and ready for all eventualities. But they were to be disappointed once more when Noel hove into view. 'Hello Lads', he called out to them in a clear and steady voice. 'What can I do for you?' They said they were here to rob him and that he was to hand over his money immediately. Well, at least Andy said so, for as well a being leader, he was the best at accents. He issued the instructions in as close as he could get to a New York heavies accent. But, since he had never been to New York, he was not at all sure that it sounded right. In any case, Noel understood what it was they wanted, and went to put his hand into his pocket to retrieve the cash that was hidden in there.

'Hold it', said a voice, 'no funny business. What have you got in your pocket?'

'I am not armed', replied Noel, whose most offensive weapon was a comb he used on his receding hair to keep it in as fine a fettle as he could manage. 'I'm just getting out the wallet of notes for you. I suppose you'll leave me with the loose coins? I need to get some petrol in the car on the way home. Bad enough to be robbed but I don't want to have to walk home as well for the want of a few drops of juice.'

The criminals looked at one another. Each nodded in turn. Andy said it was alright to hold on to the change;

but asked if the bank notes weren't marked in some way. 'The only marks that could be on them are the tears some of them shed when they parted with them', said Noel who was by now wondering if he should just walk away to his car with the money and leave them wondering what their next move might be.

'Hand over the notes', said Andy who was by now making the executive decisions. Noel did so. 'Thanks', said Andy, who was unsure of the protocol to be followed in such matters. 'You're welcome', said Noel. 'Can I go now?' They said yes and he drove straight to the Garda station.

The four robbers took off their balaclavas and boiler suits, placed them in a large black plastic refuse bag and headed for Brian's house to split up the loot. Brian had thoughtfully bought a number of beers for a celebratory drink. As planned, they dumped the bag in a clothing recycling bin before they arrived at Brian's. The haul was large for they had landed on a collection that was the end of a week and the end of a month, and therefore Noel had collected from both weekly and monthly accounts. All of the money he had collected throughout the day was now piled up on a table in Brian's house and the gang of four wondered just how much riches there was now before them.

It was hardly a king's ransom. It was, after all, simply the sum total of one man's efforts on behalf of his employer. But to the four teenagers who had never seen as much real cash as this in their lives, it was a fortune to be carefully counted but wildly spent. While they were considering what they would spend their share on, the doorbell rang. Outside at the front, were the gardaí and outside at the back were the gardaí. Before long the four robbers were in custody in the Garda station.

They didn't understand how they were caught. Andy was the most perplexed of them all. He pointed out to the arresting officer that they had worn masks and boiler suits and could not have been recognised. That was correct allowed the officer, but while all four were excellently disguised as criminals are in such robberies, the dog was not masked. The same dog had bitten Noel the week before, when he called to Brian's house for payment of the arrears on the television rent. So Noel could easily identify the four pals who were now also failed criminals. As he said when he regained his employer's stolen cash, 'Once bitten never forgotten. On television or off.'

20

THE DOLOCHER

The image of a black dog is a powerful one in Dublin storytelling. The black dog is sometimes a banshee in disguise. It is sometimes a demon bent on mischief and destruction. It is sometimes the stuff of nightmares. We are conditioned by many generations of storytelling to think of the black animal as a threat to our safety, life and wellbeing.

Consider then the terror that took hold of the city when it was believed that a black four-legged animal was prowling the streets of Dublin targeting lone women, attacking them with fearful consequences as they flit fearfully along the poorly lit narrow streets. Despite many and widespread searches, no sign of the animal could be found. Safety could be assured for no person, once darkness fell.

In this case, however, the four-legged animal was not a black dog, but a black pig. While pigs wandered freely through the streets of eighteenth-century Dublin, the Dolocher was different. It prowled the night and it attacked without warning. The belief was that the beast was the ghost of a convicted murderer and rapist, who had committed suicide in the Black Dog Jail that stood in the Cornmarket area of the city. The jail was a debtors' prison, governed and managed by deeply corrupt officials and guards. Unfortunate debtors had to pay their jailers for sufficient food, drink and bedding to stay alive until their debts were cleared. There were also people who had been sentenced to death in this prison, which was not unusual at this time. Prisoners were dispatched by public execution, both to chastise the wrongdoer and as a warning to others of a similar fate should they transgress.

A convict by the name of Olocher was lodged in this prison, under sentence of death for rape and murder. Olocher was to be hanged by the neck until he was dead. The convicted Olocher thought it better to take his own life before being publicly executed on Gallows Green before a mocking crowd. On the night before his execution, Olocher cut his own throat with a knife given to him by a sentry. Such a swift end would have been soon forgotten, except that it was soon after this death that a reign of terror began in Dublin.

It was reported that something in the form of a black pig began assaulting sentries, in the first instance, then lone women in the darkness of night. Terror spread through Dublin when the sentry whose station was at the top of a long flight of steps that led into Cook Street below, was found lying speechless, with his unfired gun by his side. He was brought to the hospital in the adjacent jail, such as it was. In time, his senses and speech returned, but one side of his body appeared powerless as if stricken by a paralytic stroke, which he declared was caused by an apparition of a black pig which attacked him.

The next night, another sentry called out the alarm to turn out the guard. This sentry confirmed the sighting of a black pig which had attacked him. One attack followed another, night after night. The guard was called out each time. Its members declared they had seen a strangely fearsome animal of unnatural appearance. Many people of the neighbourhood affirmed the same apparition.

Terror deepened when the relief guard did its rounds of the Black Dog Prison at midnight. They visited each sentry position; but found the sentinel at one station seemed to have deserted his post. He could not be found. However, on searching behind the sentry box they saw what they believed to be the form of a man lying down. On closer inspection it was found to be the sentry's gun. It was fully accoutred with his shirt draped around it, the relief reported. The supposition was that the unfortunate man had been devoured by some animal. It was not a huge leap of the imagination to think that it was the black pig that had attacked the unfortunate sentry. He had carried him off, leaving nothing except his outer garments and his unfired gun. Many believed that it was the work of the Dolocher, who had left the mark of his revenge on a sentry for what happened to him.

Terror spread on every side, both within and without the prison. The very next day, a woman came before the magistrates to swear that she had seen the Dolocher, in nearby Christ Church Lane. It made a bite at her, she said, and it held fast her cloak with its tusks. She fled in absolute terror and left her cloak with the monster, which had already been given the name of 'The Dolocher'. These reports continued. A pregnant woman was attacked by the monster and miscarried her baby as a result.

The fright continued until no woman would venture out after nightfall, for fear of being assailed by a demon in the form of a sharp-tusked black pig, intent on maiming and harming all it met. It was now hinted that because Olocher was sentenced to death for a rape and murder, his hatred of women tormented him after his suicide, so that he was now hunting down lone women as a consequence.

A group of men banded together to rid the city of this torment. At a late hour, they combed around Cook Street and the surrounding streets and laneways for the black pig. They were armed with clubs, swords, knives, and any weapon they could lay their hands on. They were determined to slay every black pig they met so as to be sure they had killed the Dolocher.

The slaughter commenced. According to reports of the time, such a breaking of legs, fracturing of skulls, stabbing, maiming, and destroying, had never been heard of before. The streets were littered with dead and bleeding and expiring animals. At the time, Dublin was populated with so many pigs kept for food, but allowed to wander freely, that bailiffs were obliged to go through the streets demanding their owners keep them in order. Bailiffs even killed the swine with pikes, when a recalcitrant owner failed to ensure the animal was brought under control. Corpses were thrown into carts to carry them away. The hunters of the Dolocher did not bother with such niceties. They left the butchered and screaming animals where they fell.

Terrifyingly, when dawn broke after a night of slaughter, not a pig, black or otherwise, could be seen anywhere. The streets were empty when light spilled through the lanes and alleyways that had been so cloaked by darkness the night before. The absence of slain bodies was attributed by a hysterical population to some infernal agency at work in removing the carcasses in the same way that the corpse of the sentry had disappeared from his post. However, when no further sightings of the Dolocher were reported that winter, nor in the longer days that followed, it was thought he must have fallen in the massacre, even though he was said to be a ghost in the first place.

Those who owned and lost a pig, even if they had but one, did not show much regret, as it had fallen in the glorious effort that had delivered the city from a plague. Nonetheless, when the days shortened once more and darkness stretched through the streets for longer and longer each night, the Dolocher re-appeared. A young woman passing by Fisher's Alley on Wood Quay was pulled in and a bundle of clothes that she carried in her hand was dragged from her, as was her cloak. The alarm spread and people grew fearful once more. Women fled from the streets, especially about Fisher's Alley, Christ Church Lane and surrounding thoroughfares.

Everything must come to an end, even black terror. The story of the Dolocher drew to a conclusion quite by accident, by a simple case of mistaken identity. A country blacksmith came into Dublin on business. As befitted his occupation, he was a brawny man with a fist as strong as a smith's hammer. Once his business was concluded, he had a drink or two with friends and maybe one more than he should have had for someone intent on a journey. Darkness had arrived before he prepared to return home.

It was a wet night with sweeping rain washing all before it on empty streets. The blacksmith had no greatcoat to withstand the elements on the journey that lay before him. Instead, he wrapped himself up in a woman's cloak belonging to his friend's wife, and she placed on his head an old black beaver bonnet, and out he went with jovial warnings to take care, lest he be eaten by the beast that was the Dolocher.

He was not so far advanced on his journey when out rushed a black shape ready to pounce. Despite his size, the Dolocher pinned him against the wall. The blacksmith was not a man to give in easily, and especially not with warming drink in his belly and fire in his blood. He raised his muscular arm and struck the attacking beast; down dropped the Dolocher after that single blow. The blow was followed by a number of kicks from the enraged blacksmith. By which point the attacker was screaming and frantically rolling about on the ground trying to escape. While the Dolocher groaned under the man's foot, the blacksmith called out that he had killed the Dolocher. As a crowd collected, the groaning devil that had terrorised the city of Dublin for so long was lifted up from where he lay in agony. His secret was revealed.

Out of a black pig's skin came the form of the sentry who had been supposedly carried off from his post at the Black Dog. He had invented his own disappearance and had moved only through darkness ever since. He draped the black skin about his frame when he attacked, the better to protect his identity and to increase the terror so a victim would be half defeated before he attacked at all. The Dolocher was removed to the jail hospital, where his earlier victim had been taken. The marauder died there, the next day, from a fractured skull, sustained when the blacksmith imposed his swift and painful justice on him.

Before his death, he confessed that Olocher, the prisoner, had committed suicide with his assistance. He further revealed he was the ringleader in the disposing of the pigs, and that as fast as they were killed they were removed by accomplices to a cellar in Schoolhouse Lane. He did so to profit from the pork so cheaply provided by the vigilantes, but also so that it appeared they had been moved by ghostly hands. Such strange goings-on would ensure that fear of the terrible being that prowled the streets of Dublin continued.

In this way, he had kept up the myth of the Black Pig of Dublin for the purpose of robbery and assault. The Dolocher has not been seen in Dublin for hundreds of years, but they say his spirit lives on in dark corners of dark streets when winter nights cause people to hurry on about their business, towards the safety of home and away from dark corners where strange beings may lurk.

21

THE AJAX DOG

While man may tremble and shiver with fear and apprehension in the face of storms and the awful majesty of the aroused heavens, often a man's dog comes to the fore in such adversity. Sometimes the spirit of that dog lingers on past its own demise to remind us of what was.

Many are the accounts of a spectral canine being seen long after the animal and its master have come to the end of their lives on this earth. Such a ghost dog was reportedly seen in Dublin, for almost a century after the tragic drowning of his master. He was seen by some in St Patrick's Cathedral, by others in a nearby graveyard. The black Labrador simply refused to accept the consequence of the events off the coast of County Dublin in early February 1861.

Dublin and the east coast experienced some fierce storms in the early 1860s. One such storm brought snow to the Dublin Mountains above the coast, where deep drifts were the order of the day. The townland where Malachi Horan the storyteller lived on his family farm did not escape this storm. The story was collected by Dr George Aloysius Little in his book *Malachi Horan Remembers Rathfarnham and Tallaght in the Nineteenth Century*.

The family woke one morning to find their home in pitch darkness. There was a terrible hush over the house. Snow had fallen overnight to cover the small cottage to the height of the chimney outside. There were fifty-foot drifts on the mountain that had not been there the night before. The Horan sheep were somewhere under that snow. They were completely invisible to the human eye. Shep, their dog, went hunting for the lost flock with young Malachi. As they walked, their feet sank deep into the soft whiteness that surrounded them. It was bitterly cold with the wind bringing frozen air from the Russian Steppes across the continent of Europe to the east.

Shep soon found the air holes that were kept open by the warm breath of the ewes that indicated life to the searchers. Once they had come upon signs of the lost sheep, the rescuers dug with frozen hands and throbbing fingers to locate the terrified and bucking animals and drag them out by the shoulders from their suffocating prison of snow. Temperatures were so cold on the side of the mountain that the air hurt Horan's chest when he drew breath into his lungs. They were fortunate that they lost but ten of the flock when the rescue was done, and the traumatised animals were drawn closer in for safety.

They were so blessed for Malachi's father Pat Horan had divined on the previous day that snow was on the way. He had sent the boy and Shep out as a precaution to bring the sheep in closer to the house. Horan was a man of the land, in tune with the earth and the elements. He was well aware that a storm was on its way. Farmers and sailors alike had long read the elements for signs of changes in the weather. Operational meteorology only began in Ireland from October 1860, when the first real-time weather observation was transmitted from Valentia Island in County Kerry. The Valentia Observatory was one of a network of weather stations established around the coastlines by the naval authorities in London, to enable storm warnings to be provided for ships at sea.

Such warnings notwithstanding, man still had to face whatever the elements chose to visit upon him and to try to protect life and property as best he could. On the night of Friday, 8 February 1861, one of the worst gales ever recorded sprung up in the Irish Sea, hitting shipping and vessels all the way from Bray in County Wicklow up to Drogheda in County Louth. Some 135 vessels sank during the storm, thirteen of them went down in the region of Dún Laoghaire Harbour alone.

On the following morning, the people of Dún Laoghaire awoke to find their harbour filled with debris and wreckage from boats that foundered in the storm and were now thrown ashore in bits and pieces. Dozens of bodies of drowned mariners and others were taken from the water and laid out in sorrowful lines on dry land. At sea, the waves still rolled on in the aftermath of the storm, while falling snow, sleet and rain reduced visibility and chilled the hands, feet and faces of the rescuers.

Among the wailing, searching, grappling and dragging of the wreckage, the crew of the Royal Naval coastguard ship, *Ajax*, under Captain John McNeill Boyd went about their duties. The Royal Navy maintained a constant presence in Dún Laoghaire, then called Kingstown, all year round. HMS *Ajax* was on station from 1858 until 1864. Built in 1809 as a seventy-four gun wooden ship of the line; she was described as being like many that fought at Trafalgar under Nelson. The *Ajax* was fitted with an auxiliary steam engine in 1846. However, she was noted for her poor performance under both sail and steam. Paradoxically, Boyd and his men were to be drowned from dry land while attempting a marine rescue of fellow sailors.

On the fateful day, when even more men joined the drowned of the night before, it was reported that three stricken vessels the *Neptune*, the *Industry* and the *Mary*, carrying cargoes of coal from Britain, were making for the safety of the harbour. Fierce winds conspired to sweep them towards the treacherous rocks off the East Pier. They could not make safety, no matter what their level of maritime skill or what they did to correct their course. Boyd and his sailors, along with officers and men of the Kingstown district coastguard, hurried towards the rocks to attempt to save some of the unfortunate men from the ships when they struck. It being still winter time with temperatures well down below comfort, many of the rescuers were dressed in heavy clothing. Witnesses said Boyd himself was encumbered by his greatcoat, and started to take it off so as to move easier in the tough conditions. But as he did so, a large wave, as high as a mountain, crashed over him and his men, and they disappeared into the churning waters along with everyone else that had been standing there.

In the event, two of the vessels, the *Neptune* and the *Industry*, from Whitehaven, were wrecked within 100 yards of each other with great loss of life. The third ship, the *Mary*, was swept on to Sandymount a distance away to the north of the others where it was also wrecked. The bodies of Boyd and his men were not recovered from the sea for some days, despite extensive searches by boats and the crew of the *Ajax* and other searchers. Lost with Boyd were: Able Seamen John Curry and Thomas Murray; Ordinary Seamen John Russell, James Johnson and Alexander Forsythe.

When some calm returned and a lifeboat from the *Ajax* patrolled the waters, observers saw the captain's black dog sat in the prow, desperately seeking its companion and master. The bodies of the crewmen were washed ashore days later, but the sea was not to give up the body of the courageous Boyd for weeks.

The remains of the crew members of the *Ajax* were buried in the graveyard at Carrickbrennan in Monkstown, near Dún Laoghaire. While his companions were buried near to the events of the day, Boyd's remains were interred in the grounds of St Patrick's Cathedral, in Dublin city, where a memorial was erected within the Cathedral to him. His body was brought to the cathedral in funeral procession. It was reportedly one of the biggest funerals seen in Dublin, with thousands of people walking in the cortege.

Many noticed that the captain's dog walked behind the hearse. It stayed close to Boyd as his body lay in state in the Cathedral. The dog sat as if waiting its master's call to sail the seas once more, a call that was not to come. When the remains were brought to the graveyard to be buried, the dog followed it to the graveside. Even when the solemn ceremonies had ended, and the grave was filled in, the dog remained with its master. It lay on top of the grave and refused to leave, eventually expiring of hunger, despite attempts to entice it away or to get it to eat. Another life ended, in an ongoing tragedy.

Then, a strange thing happened that few could explain, but that is still spoken of to this day in Dublin. A memorial statue was erected in St Patrick's Cathedral by the citizens of Dublin to the memory of Captain Boyd. The inscription on the statue reads, 'Erected by the citizens of Dublin, to the memory of John McNeill Boyd, R.N., Captain, H.M.S. Ajax, born Londonderry, 1812, and lost off the rocks at Kingstown, February 9th, 1861, attempting to save the crew of the Brig, Neptune.' In the time that followed, the shadowy figure of a dog was seen at night, sitting at the base of the statue, and at other times by the grave of the drowned sailor. The last person on record said to have seen the ghost dog died in 1950.

Boyd was posthumously awarded the Sea Gallantry Medal in silver, the RNLI silver medal and the Tayleur Fund medal in gold for his rescue actions that day. The RNLI citation read how Captain Boyd then serving in the screw steamer HMS *Ajax*, assisted in saving the crew of the brig *Neptune* wrecked during a heavy gale on the East Pier of Kingstown, County Dublin. The silver medal, accompanied by a letter of condolence, was presented to his widow Cordelia. His inscription in St Patrick's Cathedral reads:

Safe from the rocks,
Whence swept thy manly form
The tide white rush,
The stepping of the storm.
Borne with a public pomp,
By just decree
Heroic sailor!
From that fatal sea.
A city vows this marble unto thee,
And here in this calm place, where never sin
of earth great waterfloods shall enter in.
When to our human hearts, two thoughts are given,
One, Christ's self-sacrifice, the other heaven.
Here is it meet for grief and love to grave
The Christ-taught bravery that died to save
The life not lost but found beneath the wave.
All Thy billows and Thy Waves passed over me, yet
I will look again toward Thy Holy Temple.
There is no memorial to his faithful dog who was steadfast
both in life and in death. But he stayed true, public
memorial or no.

22

LITTLE JOHN IN DUBLIN

Even outlaws like to go on holiday.

It seems that John Little or Little John of Sherwood Forest, who was reputedly one of the most famous outlaws in England in his day, came to Dublin to visit some of the local vagabonds and to inspect the caves around Arbour Hill, situated near the present day Phoenix Park. He did so when his glory days as an outlaw in England had ended.

But unlike most visitors to the city, he was never to leave Dublin again. Instead, he was hanged for his misdeeds in Dublin some time in the twelfth century, according to local legend.

Gilbert's *History of the City of Dublin* suggested that Little John, second in command to the romantic outlaw Robin Hood, travelled to Dublin and Oxmantown when Robin and his band of merry men were finally disbanded. It's a plausible enough story, given that there had long been trade between England and Ireland by sea. Little John, and anyone else that cared to travel with him, could easily have travelled to Dublin on a trading ship.

Once arrived, he would have found the terrain to the north of the river not unfamiliar to his eye. While there would not have been the vast forests of oak trees he was accustomed to hanging out in, many caves dotted the terrain. The great oak forest that used to stand at Arbour

Hill had been cut down and shipped to London, where at least some of it found its way into the roof timbers of Westminster Abbey. But great roots still lay beneath the soil.

Beneath the land at Arbour Hill lay a labyrinth of caverns, much used by thieves and others to escape into and to conceal their stolen goods from pursuers. Back in Little John's hunting ground at Nottingham, the castle sat on an easily-defended cliff above a network of sandstone caves below. Indeed, there were many caves, hills, and wooded areas of concealment in and around the area of Sherwood Forest which in Little John's time stretched for a distance of some twenty miles.

A story lingers on in Dublin that the visiting outlaw fired an arrow from his long bow, a distance of some 700 metres, from the only bridge the crossed the Liffey at the time upwards towards Arbour Hill. Whether this was to show his accuracy with the weapon of choice of the Merry Men back home or simply to re-enforce his mystique as a mighty man is lost in time. It might even have been as part of a wager. Certainly, the locals would have encouraged any stranger to show his mettle, for a Dubliner likes to take the measure of a visitor.

It is interesting how the Dublin story features Little John standing on a bridge to draw his longbow, when stories of his first encounter with Robin Hood involve Little John trying to prevent Robin from crossing a narrow bridge. The two are said to have fought one another with hardwood quarter staves, with Robin being knocked into the river by his opponent when he lost the stick fight. Despite being the victor of the battle, John Little is said to have agreed to join Robin's band and to be subservient to him. That he was reputedly a giant of a man standing some seven feet in height when most Dubliners would have been teetering around the five-foot mark, would have made him stand out even more. But, who knows how tall he was, for height is often a matter of subjective comment. If someone defeated

a warrior from another country, he would of course have been a worthy opponent and taller in the telling. Conversely, if the head was still ringing from the pummelling received, the loser would doubtless swear it was a giant of man that beat him despite his best and heroic efforts to fight his corner.

The old bridge from which the big man shot his arrow spanned the river where the present bridge now crosses from Church Street to Bridge Street, near the Four Courts. The main road through Dublin, from Tara in County Meath to the north to Wicklow and the southern counties, crossed the Liffey at this point. If Little John had lived a few centuries later, he could have shown his expertise in shooting deer in the new royal deer park at Phoenix Park beside the cave area, but that was not to be formed until the seventeenth century, when his visit had already faded into local lore.

The county gallows was moved away from modern Parkgate Street to Kilmainham, south of the river, to make way for a grand entrance to the park in the 1600s. Thieves and others were still hanged in public gaze. However, even after the removal of the gallows, the end result was much the same if it was your day for the hangman to greet you with a rope necklace.

If he was in the city as a type of consultant, then perhaps Little John joined local brigands in robbing and relieving travellers and merchants of their goods as they passed along towards the single Liffey bridge. Perhaps the English outlaw in Dublin might even have been an impostor living on the

legend of Little John. Whatever the truth of the story, someone was caught and duly hanged for his troubles.

This man, impostor or not, was hanged at Gibbet's
Glade, a place of public execution for criminals. We do not
know what happened to his body afterwards. Being hanged
from a gibbet as a punishment usually meant the dead body
was left to hang in the air for as long as the authorities saw
fit, as warning to all. Sometimes, they swung there until
their clothes rotted away; sometimes it was until the body
decomposed. People said it made a mournful sound, when
a dead man swung in the wind, waiting for his body to rot
while crows pecked away at what was left. It made little difference to the deceased for he was past caring what was done
to his person.

Otherwise, it was the custom of the hangman to toss the
dead bodies of his charges into a nearby pit prepared for the
purpose. So perhaps Little John joined other not-so-merry
corpses in a hole in the ground somewhere on the northside
of Dublin.

Except ...

Little John's fame and last resting place is claimed by
the town of Hathersage in Derbyshire, England. It is also
claimed that he was born there. A memorial tells us that
Little John died in a cottage to the east of the churchyard.
To complicate matters, the cottage is now said to have been
destroyed at some time in the past. If Little John died in
Derbyshire, then the Dublin impostor surely got a raw deal
when he was hanged as someone else on the public gallows.
Though it may have been rough justice, since the condemned man was undoubtedly a thief and lived in a time
of savagery among thieves and the law itself, which hanged
citizens for less reason than would be tolerated now.

Oxmantown and the area of Arbour Hill that Little
John may have roamed through was for a long time treated
as a separate part of Dublin, being, as it was, across the
river from the seat of power and somewhat bordering the

countryside. It served as a market and trading area for people from outside the city who brought animals and goods to Dublin for sale and trade. With so many people coming and going and buying and selling goods, it was no wonder that thieves were attracted to this place to prey on those weaker than themselves and to rob them of the proceeds of their day's trading.

Later on, a thief known as Scaldbrother caused no little heartache for the people of the area. The sixteenth-century bandit roamed far and wide accosting local and visitor alike. He fled with their valuables into the huge maze of underground passages extending for some two miles beneath the ground, from the hay market at Smithfield to Arbour Hill where livestock was bought and sold on market day.

Not content with being a very successful thief, Scaldbrother was also a champion runner in a time when the watchmen were still on foot. It was their task to preserve the peace and to protect the citizenry. No matter who tried to catch him or who challenged him in his swift flight, Scaldbrother was always able to outrun and outlast them. So brazen did he become, that the running thief began mocking his pursuers for their slowness. It was even said that he would halt beside the Gallows tavern and pretend to place a rope around his neck and play at hanging himself in full view of his expiring pursuers. As some chasers grew close, he ran on to his underground hideout in the caves where no one would dare pursue him.

While his exploits were hailed among the criminal fraternity as reckless and daring, there was to be a reckoning for Scaldbrother from civilised society, as there had been for the man who called himself Little John of Sherwood Forest. As the hare, in the tale of the hare and the tortoise, had long since discovered slow but steady wins the race. A plan was hatched to best Scaldbrother by stratagem rather than speed. A number of stout young men, known for their speed and strength, were chosen to wait in ambush along his habitual escape route. The next time he came by, running from his pursuers, he ran straight into the arms of his captors who lost no time in bundling him away to justice. Scaldbrother, the errant robber, was hanged on the very next day for his misdeeds. His execution was in public. Many of his victims would have attended to witness the end of the scourge that was Scaldbrother. He would run through the caves of Dublin no more. His race, along with Little John's, was run.

23

TRAGEDY ON IRELAND'S EYE

In the early autumn of 1852, a married couple journeyed by boat to Ireland's Eye off Howth for a day's enjoyment. Just one of them was to come back alive. He was then to serve some twenty-seven years imprisonment on a prison island in Cork Harbour, for the murder of his wife on that day. Opinion in Dublin was split as his arrest and trial proceeded. Some said the woman died of natural causes, others said the man killed her.

William Burke Kirwan was sentenced to death for the murder of his wife, Sarah Maria Louisa Kirwan, whom he called Maria. However, the sentence was commuted to imprisonment on Spike Island in Cork Harbour. Kirwan was to be the last prisoner released from that prison in 1883 when Spike Island changed its custodial use to that of a purely military post. He was said to have been a professional artist and anatomical draughtsman. He was aged about thirty at the time of his wife's death. He was residing on Merrion Street with Sarah to whom he had been married for some twelve years. He was also believed, by neighbours at a Sandymount house, about a mile away from Merrion Street, to be the husband of a Miss Mary Kenny who lived there with seven of their children and who also used the name of Mrs Kirwan at times.

Sarah Kirwan was well-made and extremely good-looking. She was about thirty-five years of age when she died. She was fond of swimming in the sea, and was a powerful and daring swimmer, according to witnesses. Therefore it was considered doubtful that she could have drowned by accident.

The story was that the Kirwans took lodgings with Mrs Power in Howth, where William sketched and Sarah swam in her bathing dress. At 10 a.m. on Monday 6 September, they took a boat to the island of Ireland's Eye, carrying Mrs Kirwan's bathing dress, a basket of provisions, two bottles of water and a sketch-book. It was the custom for boatmen to discharge their passengers and to go back to the island in the evening in order to return their passengers to Howth Harbour.

Another couple, a Mr and Mrs Brue, testified that they had landed on the island on the same day. Mrs Brue said that when she was leaving at about 4 p.m. she offered Mrs Kirwan a seat in her boat, but Mrs Kirwan declined the offer. Whatever befell Sarah Kirwan occurred in the following hours, when she and her husband were alone on the island. Several witnesses testified they heard repeated cries coming from the island, shortly after the Brues landed at Howth, not long after 4 p.m.. A rain shower fell at around 6 p.m. When four boatmen travelled at 8 p.m. to collect the couple, they found Kirwan standing alone on a high rock above the landing place. He said his wife left his company after the shower, and he had not seen her since.

After a prolonged search, one of the boatmen found Sarah Kirwan's body on a sheet, on a rock, in the middle of an area known as the Long Hole, the very area that witnesses said the cries had emanated from earlier in the day. The court heard that the rock was dry and the tide had receded six feet from its base by the time the boatmen had arrived. The dead woman was lying on her back on the rock with her bathing chemise drawn up from her body.

Kirwan showed signs of distress and told the boatmen to go and fetch her clothes. When the boatmen could not find her clothes Kirwan left them and returned a little later, to tell them where to find the clothes. Boatman

Patrick Nagle testified that he then found the clothes in a place where, as he swore to the court, he had already searched without success.

The woman's body was wrapped in a sail and brought back to Howth. It was noted that there were scratches on the face and eyelids, and blood came from a cut on the breast, and from the ears. An inquest returned the verdict that she had drowned, and the body was buried in Glasnevin Cemetery. Nevertheless, rumours of foul play began to circulate. It was said that Kirwan had murdered his wife, a concept apparently supported by the existence of seven offspring with another woman. Kirwan was arrested and charged with the murder of Sarah, in December of the same year.

At his trial, an expert witness said the tide was full at about 3 p.m. that day. At about 6.30 p.m., the time Kirwan said Sarah left him to swim, after the shower, there were about three feet six inches of water over the rock. By 9.30 p.m., when the body was found, the water was about two feet lower than the rock. It is about half a mile from where the body was found to the island's landing place. George Hatchel, an MD and surgeon, testified that on an examination of the body, when it had been exhumed thirty-one days after death, he discovered no internal or external trace of violence. He was of the opinion that death was caused by asphyxia or stoppage of the respiration and that stoppage of respiration must have been combined with pressure or constriction of some kind. Simple drowning would not have caused the appearance presented. Going into the water with a full stomach would be likely to cause a fit, he said. Dr Hatchel said that marks on the eye-lids and on the breasts could have been caused by sea crabs attacking the body.

Kirwan's defence argued that if he had followed his wife into the water and held her under, then his arms and body must have been as wet as his feet were when the boatmen arrived on that evening. Kirwan said his footwear was damp from walking across wet grass on the island searching for his missing wife. Surgeon Rynd swore that, in his opinion, the appearance of the body at the post-mortem examination would be produced by an epileptic fit that could have resulted from sudden immersion in water with a full stomach.

However, when prosecutors asked if placing a wet sheet over the mouth and nose would produce all the effects of drowning, medical witnesses said it would be impossible, by the appearances described, to distinguish between accidental or forcible drowning. Once all the witnesses had been heard, Mr Justice Crampton charged the jury and they retired. At 7.40 p.m. they returned. The foreman reported that he didn't think they were likely to agree. A second juror said there was not the most remote chance of them agreeing. When a third juror said there was not the smallest chance of an agreement, the Justice said he would return at 11 p.m. to see how they were getting on. When he heard then that there was no verdict, he said it would be necessary for them to remain in the room for the night without food.

After a further half-an-hour's deliberation, they returned with a guilty verdict. Kirwan continued to declare his innocence, even when the sentence of death was pronounced by the judge. The death sentence was commuted, by the then Lord Lieutenant Lord Eglinton, who was the head of government in Ireland under the Crown system. Kirwan was ordered to serve penal servitude for life. He was removed to Spike Island, where he served no less than twenty-seven years imprisonment to his release on 3 March 1879. His release was conditional on his going to live outside the British dominions.

It was said he travelled to the United States, in search of the mother of his seven children who had migrated there when the trial was completed. In his defence, those who said Kirwan was an innocent man said it was extremely unlikely that he could have followed Sarah into the water and drowned her with his hands or with a wet sheet without either of them showing marks of a struggle on their bodies. The theory of accidental drowning while undergoing a fit induced by entering the water with a full stomach, met all the facts of the case, it was argued by M. McDonnell Bodkin, K.C. author of the 1918 *Famous Irish Trials*.

A pamphlet *The Ireland's Eye Tragedy* by J. Knight Boswell was published in 1853. The pamphlet alleged that suspicion was aroused against Kirwan by information made on 21 September 1852, by a Mrs Byrne, who carried a bitter grudge against Kirwan, and who constantly strove to make trouble between him and his wife. She said she believed that Kirwan had taken his wife to some strange place to destroy her, and she had no doubt in her mind that the said Mrs Kirwan was wilfully drowned by her husband.

Mrs Crowe, Sarah Kirwan's mother, contradicted this allegation when she said there could not be a quieter husband than Kirwan was to her daughter. Indeed, servants in the Kirwan household all deposed that Mrs Kirwan was subject to fits. One, Ellen Malone, said that on one occasion, Mrs Kirwan told her she felt her senses leaving her while sitting in a tin bath of lukewarm water. Malone said she saw Sarah's face suddenly turn pale, and she became insensible.

McDonnell Bodkin quoted a Dr Taylor, who in February 1853, minutely examined the evidence in the light of medical authority and example, and of his own personal experience, and concluded by declaring:

> There is an entire absence of proof that death is the result of violence at the hands of another. Persons bathing or exposed to the chance of drowning are often seized with fits which may prove suddenly fatal, though they may allow of a short struggle. The fit may arise from syncope, apoplexy, or epilepsy, either of the last conditions would explain all the medical circumstances in this remarkable case.

Furthermore, experts said the resistance which a vigorous person can offer to a murderer intent on drowning her is such as to lead to a necessity to inflict greater violence than is necessary to ensure death of the victim. The absence of any marks of violence or wounds on the body of Mrs Kirwan suggested that death was not the result of homicidal drowning or suffocation, but most probably from a fit resulting from natural causes. Kirwan's real offence would appear to have been against morality, his defenders suggested. It was clear from reports of the trial that at least some of the jury were reluctant to convict. It was only on what amounted to a threat that they would be locked up all night without food that they produced a guilty verdict.

A twist in the tale came when it was revealed by John Wynn, Secretary to the Lord Lieutenant, the Earl of Eglinton, that:

> … in commuting the death sentence passed on Mr Kirwan, Lord Eglinton acted on the recommendation of Judge Crampton and Baron Green, with the concurrence of the Lord Chancellor, and he neither solicited nor received the advice of any other person whatsoever.

Guilty of murder, or guilty of transgressing the moral code of the day, William Burke Kirwan's life took a turn for the worse on that September day on Ireland's Eye in 1852, when he and his wife stepped ashore on Ireland's Eye, and their marriage disappeared forever.

24

DEAD CAT BOUNCE

Who knows what goes on in a cat's mind? They pay lip service to man, but leave as soon as the call comes from their kin, day or night. They return when it suits them and devil a one knows what transpired while they were away.

There is a story that is told in many ways and in many countries of a man that witnessed hordes of cats burying the king cat, with a great torch-lit ceremony one pitch black night. Often, when the story is told in the presence of a cat, he will listen attentively to the end of the tale where the king cat is declared dead. Then, the formerly silent animal attacks the teller or races away declaring itself to be the new king of the cats.

A story is told of a meeting of cats on the road near Tallaght in County Dublin. They were there, it was said, to elect a new king. In the suffocating darkness, a man, with drink on him and in charge of an ass and cart, drove through them. He killed so many cats that locals swept barrowfuls of them off the road, the next morning. The now sober man did not sleep for weeks afterwards for fear the watching, hating cats would tear his throat open in revenge if he fell asleep. His only solution was to buy a pair of terriers that he loosed on the cats until they were dispersed to the four winds. Whatever evil eye had been placed on him for killing cats, with the wheels of his cart, was finally sent away to another parish. What happened to him when the dogs grew old and slow and the descendants of the vengeful cats returned we do not know. But ever afterwards he walked with a permanent twist in his neck from looking over his shoulder. If he saw a big buck cat on the path ahead of him, he always crossed the road to be away from it.

Another man in the county of Dublin had cause to wonder at the mortality of cats. He wondered how many lives a cat really had after what happened to him on the high descent down a steep hill in the valley of the Liffey. Clem lived all his life in the valley not far from Dublin City. To get to the nearest town he had to climb up one hill, pushing his bicycle by the saddle and walking freely beside it. Once there, he freewheeled down the far side to the shops and the bookies in the nearest village.

When he was out of puff from pushing the old black Raleigh bicycle with the well sprung Brooks saddle on it up one hill, he freewheeled down the other side without bothering with brakes at all. This was no major decision to make for the bike had no brakes at all left on it. The brake block shivered and shuddered and eventually ceased to greet the rim of the wheel at all. In any case, Clem leaned into the corners mightily on the way down and took the entire width of the road when necessary to gather speed on a sharp bend. On the odd day when he slowed his descent, he leant backwards and rubbed the side of his boot on the rim of the front wheel to slow down. Such was the way he progressed and no harm ever came to him over it. He even had time to whoop at people he knew as he whizzed past them on his way downhill.

One day, a neighbour woman asked him to drown a dead cat for her. The cat was a family pet, she explained, and she did not want to throw it away herself in her grief. Clem was a little taken aback, for he had only called in to see if she knew whether the milkman was on holidays or not or had someone stolen the milk from his door early that morning.

He suspected the neighbour herself to be the milk thief, but would never say so. At one time, it was perfectly acceptable to drop animals into the river, where they floated away as a passing treat for local water rats. The woman was an old friend of his departed mother so he agreed.

You would think it would be an easy task, to peg a tied plastic bag with a dead cat inside it into the river, but no. Every time Clem approached the river bank, there was some-one about, and this stayed his hand, for he did not want to be seen throwing dead cats about the place, for he too was aware of the strange confraternity that made cats the unsettling presence they are, when they take a mind to watch your every movement. He did not want to be the target of vengeful cats, lurking along the dark road at night. When he tried to dispose of the cat under the cover of darkness, there was always a constant steam of cars coming along the road with their headlights on. So, he brought the cat home and left it in the back scullery of his house in the red fertiliser plastic bag while he waited for a better time to present itself. It stayed there for a few days while he forgot about such considerations in favour of a more pressing matter, that was, the form of three racehorses that were running on Saturday in three different races.

If he placed a bet on the first, with the winnings going onto the second, and the winnings of that being placed on the third horse, and if that horse won, he would have a small fortune to vex him with the spending of it. He discussed these matters with knowledgeable men in the run up to the event. Those that mooned it with him, over a glass or two at his home, were Christian enough not to mention the pervasive smell of recent death hanging about the house. Clem eventually noticed it on the Saturday of his big betting coup, for he could not avoid it any more. It was a powerful smell and if the rats from surrounding townlands had not yet arrived to feast on the desiccated cat, it was only because they had sent invitations to their cousins to join them and they were waiting for them to arrive to begin the festivities.

Clem was faced with a dilemma. He needed to get to town to the bookies to place the first bet as soon as possible, but it was obvious the dead cat had outstayed its welcome. It might not be safe to leave it here in his house, for a passing stranger might call the Garda to report the scent of a rotting body. Clem was not sure, but he thought there might be a rule about keeping unburied bodies on your premises for too long. He would do away with it now. No time like the present.

He pumped up the tyres of the bike to achieve more speed. He tucked his trousers into his tan socks and zipped up his good green anorak so that it would not cause counter momentum by filling with air on the descent. When he was ready, he walked out to the road with the bagged cat in one hand and his Raleigh bike in the other. Just as he was about to lob the burden into the flooded river, he saw the cat's sorrowful owner coming down the road towards him. She thought the cat was gone long before and here it was inside a bag swinging from Clem's hand. Clem unzipped his jacket just enough to stuff the stinking cat inside, next to his clean canary-yellow shirt, before the neighbour passed by with a sweet if sorrowful smile with her head to one side like it was burdened with sorrow on the one side.

The time was, by now, very close to the off in the first race. Clem threw caution to the wind. He threw his longest leg over the bar of the bike and away with him towards the town and the bookmakers. He remembered there was a builders' skip on the way into town and he wondered why he hadn't used it for disposing of his charge before this. If he kept the jacket zipped, people might think he had put on weight and was filling out the jacket more than he used. He pedalled fast and was sweating with his excess baggage and the excitement, and the exertion of rushing along to his certain fortune by the time he crested the hill. He peddled as fast as he could between the tops of the two hills and then let her freewheel down the road on the other side. Clem knew he was faster when he allowed the machine to gather its own momentum. Besides, he needed his feet free to double as brakes if something came amiss.

It was then that a strange and disturbing thing happened. The cat made its move. Clem had just rounded the final chicane, when he felt a movement above his hips and below his perspiring chest. The three racehorses together could not have sweated as much as Clem did when he felt movement. The dead cat slid its way out of the bag onto his lap as if he were sitting down. In that moment, Clem thought the frozen blood of the cat had warmed up and it had used one of its nine lives to come back to torment him. He tried to slow down as best he could, with his shaking foot, but his foot brake missed the wheel and ploughed straight into the tumbling spokes. This pitched Clem straight over the handlebars and onto the road's cold hard and ugly surface.

It was assumed afterwards that the cat they found under him had run out in front of Clem to be killed. But they said also that the suicidal cat had saved Clem's life as Clem bounced on the dead cat on his descent to earth. Clem had to have sixteen stitches put into his face to draw it back together. The Raleigh bike with its Brooks saddle was wrecked. The cat was dead for the second time, though someone threw it into the skip afterwards so it might have just been sleeping or even playing a game with Clem, much as a hunting cat will play with a mouse it is about to kill.

And what of the treble wager that Clem was racing to and almost lost his life over? Well the first horse lost and the accumulator bet didn't work out, as a result. It stopped dead there and then. No win, no second wager. Because Clem never got to the bookies, he still had his wager in his pocket when he came home from hospital. For ages afterwards he retold the story to anyone that asked him how he had acquired the scar on his face where he had been stitched.

But as the wound faded, so too did the questions, and Clem went back to normal life on his replacement bicycle. However, neighbours wondered if the fall had not affected his head in some little way. He had always been an uncomplicated man, but now neighbours said he seemed to want to stop and talk to any stray cat he met on the road. People said he seemed to be trying to explain something to the cat, but that couldn't be right, could it? For who talks to cats in daylight anyway?

25

PHOENIX PARK, NORTH STRAND BOMBING

Irish budgies could have beaten German bomber pilots at their own game, according to some Dublin know-alls. While the whole world was at war in the early 1940s, Ireland, on account of it being neutral in such matters, declared itself to be having just a bit of an Emergency.

Even so, life carried on as best it could in the capital city. Lots of products were rationed and as a result life became more difficult for most people. But, it was especially diffi-cult for the people living in the North Strand area at the close of May 1941, when German bombs came from the night sky and took away the lives of unsuspecting citizens and maimed many more. Some twenty-eight people died and ninety were injured. Three hundred houses were dam-aged or destroyed by the time the crashing of bombs and their shrieking aftermath ended their dreadful careering through the still small residential streets of Dublin early on that Saturday morning. More than 400 people were made homeless in a swoop that has been burnt into Dublin memory ever since. Some say the German bombs fell on Dublin as a result of bad navigation; others said it was retali-ation for Dublin Fire Brigade's assistance to Belfast when the northern city was fire-bombed in mid-April of the same year. Others said it was a dumping of bombs so the aircraft could gain height after shots were fired at the aircraft from a Local Defence Forces unit, stationed on Ballyfermot Hill. One officer is said to have fired his pistol into the night sky as a warning to be gone, though it is unlikely that anyone heard it except himself, so he can hardly be blamed for what happened. Either way, three bombs landed on North Strand and one on Phoenix Park where it vexed the inhabitants no end, both man and beast.

Witnesses said they heard German aircraft overhead before the bombs fell to the ground and they heard anti-aircraft fire climbing above the sleeping city in a vain attempt to protect Dublin and its people from uninvited and unwanted belligerence. Some people who heard the approaching drone barely got to the front door to look up at the sky, when bombs fell and buildings came down. People ran out. The skeletal remainder of many houses collapsed around them as they did.

Eyewitness accounts said people were thrown out of bed by the blast, while others slept through it all. One man was blown through a front door, not his own, on his way home. He and the door landed at the foot of the stairs inside the surprised household. But he made his excuses and left. Others remained where they were until rescuers came to seek the dead and the wounded, and the terrified. Clanging ambulances ferried victims to the Mater and Jervis Street hospitals where next of kin went to see what had happened to their loved ones. People used whatever tools they had to dig for survivors. Some used their hands to lift fallen masonry away. Horses and carts were used to haul debris away. Dublin had few bulldozers or heavy equipment on hand for such work. Manual labour was employed to seek for victims. Later, trucks with chains and ropes were used to pull down dangerous walls while steam rollers flattened the rubble of former homes to manageable proportions.

No sooner had summer lightened the shocked streets, than suppositions began as to the cause of it all. Belfast city and its ship-building industry had been fire-bombed

in mid-April by German bombers. The fires were so bad
in that city that the Dublin government was asked to send
fire fighting assistance northwards to tackle the blaze. It did
so, quietly and privately, for Belfast, as part of the United
Kingdom, was technically a belligerent in the war. Dublin
was not. Some twenty fire engines travelled from Dublin,
Drogheda and Dundalk with more than seventy volunteer
firemen, along with ambulances to help the victims of the
April bombings. They travelled north, once more, on 4 May
1941 when more bomb attacks were made on Belfast. This,
according to Dublin lore, made the German high command
both nervous and angry at the prospect of the Irish Free
State, as it was at the time, entering the fray, and that was
why Dublin was bombed, they said. It was a warning. Hitler
was frightened of us, they told anyone that would listen.
And he had good reason, others said without being too specific, in case there were spies about to hear what might be
the specific. Others said Dublin was mistaken for Belfast,
bombs were dropped and the airmen went home to tell fibs
to their boss Hermann Göring about where they had been.
Reports of explosions at sea, on that night, reinforce the
observation by military experts that foreign fliers jettisoned
bombs off the coast before beginning a higher altitude run
to Belfast.

No matter the cause, the first two bombs fell on North
Circular Road and on Richmond Cottages, while a third
shook the area around the Royal Canal and nearby Croke
Park in the early hours of a Whit holiday weekend morning.
While word spread through the wider city, tensions rose as
fears grew that this bombing was a prelude to an invasion of
neutral Ireland by Hitler's Germany. After all, it had been the
German battle practice, since hostilities began in Europe, to
bomb a country or city from the air as prelude to a land invasion by grey columns of thundering armour and murdering
men. As it happened, German armed forces invaded Russia
to the east the following month with full intent.

The bombing of Dublin had little to do with it, experts said, unless their pilots had flown the wrong way and a month early. Still, and to this day, Dubliners took it all very personally. Phoenix Park, where the fourth bomb landed, sits above the city and the valley of the Liffey. At the time, household water was pumped throughout the park for use by residents from a pump house beside the Dog Pond. As luck would have it, the 250-pound bomb landed close enough to the pump house to destroy it. The force of the explosion left particles of residue floating in the atmosphere for days afterwards. A crater created beside the cricket club threw up rocks that fell back to earth through the clubhouse roof. It made the grass pitch off limits because of stones strewn across the surface, a source of annoyance to the cricketers who expected to bowl and bat there as usual.

In the years that followed the defeat of Hitler's Germany, the club successfully claimed damages from the new German government for bomb damage to its roof. Damage to the zoo across the road came to £613 9s 3d in old money, before new money became old money in its turn. The Germans did not attempt a re-run of their bombing of Dublin.

The Phoenix Park bomb landed beside Dublin Zoo with its caged stock of wild and ferocious animals. There were no casualties other than broken sleep for humans and animals alike. There was general alarm that some of the animals at the zoological gardens had escaped into the public park under cover of darkness. The wild deer herd in the park numbered some 800 animals who roamed free throughout the park's 1,752 acres. They might have provided sport for wolves, lions and leopards if they had departed their lodgings in the gardens. But the zoo's perimeter held on the night, even when a maddened bison charged the restraining fence from within. Just the same, a few months later, in the month of August, the zoo's council gave an assurance that all dangerous animals would be destroyed in case of an emergency, lest they escape into the park and the city.

If, for any reason, the Germans were to have returned to threaten Dublin, the zoo had, by then, gathered together a secret air force of budgies and parrots that could have been released to cause confusion in the heads of any amount of Luftwaffe air crews. Budgies and parrots had recently been brought to the zoo by their owners for sanctuary, which is where Ireland's secret weapon comes into the story. Bird feed became scarce and hard to source in the wider community as the Second World War wore on, so where better to park pets for the duration of the Emergency than the zoo, where they would be fed and watered. In 1941, the year of the bomb, twenty-six budgies were donated by one person alone, while another bird lover brought twenty-four budgies to the zoo. Someone else handed over fifteen birds for safekeeping. It must have been a very noisy place when they were all housed and chattering away. They were there ready to answer the call to flight at any time. If there is one thing that would confuse a flying Nazi, it would be a Dublin budgie filled with the rage of the Dubs for a job badly done. It was not for nothing that German pilots might have warned one another to, 'beware of the budgies of Dublin on the way to Belfast'.

The Nazi pilots might not have been able to see in the dark but they would still have been frightened by the flying budgies of Dublin.

26

MARSH'S LIBRARY
AND THE RUNAWAY
TEENAGER

The ghost of Narcissus Marsh, a Protestant Archbishop of Dublin, is said to haunt Marsh's Library. The library is situated near the thirteenth-century St Patrick's Cathedral in the old quarter of the city, where his remains are interred. How this came about is a strange tale.

Narcissus Marsh was an Englishman who came to Ireland to work and never returned home. He was educated in Oxford and ordained in 1662. He was sent to Ireland as Provost of Trinity College Dublin in 1679. He never married and was to find the younger generation a trial, particularly his niece who it seems was to become the reason for his spectral nocturnal wanderings after his death.

While in his position at Trinity, he wrote that he was finding Dublin very troublesome, partly because of the multitude of visits the provost was obliged to carry out, and partly by reason of the ill-education that young scholars had before they came to college and were therefore both rude and ignorant. Perhaps the rudest of them all was his nineteen-year-old niece, Grace. After he had taken her in to his home, she had agreed to care of him in his old age, but then embarked on a course of independent action that vexed him sorely.

He was appointed Bishop of Ferns and Leighlin in 1683, Archbishop of Cashel in 1691, Archbishop of Dublin in

1694 and then Primate of Armagh in 1703. It was while he was Archbishop of Ireland that niece Grace struck out on her own in what was hardly an act of obeisance to such a powerful personage.

As provost of Trinity, Marsh had a new college hall and chapel built on the grounds and developed the college library. In a move to improve the efficiency of the library and its staff, Marsh insisted that when a new library keeper took up his position, an inventory of all books in his care must be presented. The following year, when a new keeper was appointed, the outgoing keeper and the new library keeper had to check that all listed books were there. If not, the outgoing keeper was charged to replace the missing books or pay in their value. Marsh acquired a good knowledge of the Irish language and encouraged the scholars to learn it. He appointed a native speaker as a lecturer to teach them the language of the country.

It was not until some twenty years later that the first public library in Ireland was built on the instructions of Archbishop Marsh and at his own cost. Designed by Sir William Robinson, it is still being used as a library 300 years later. While the books were displayed on the upper storey, the lower storey was designed as a residence for the librarian, who lived on the premises and both administered the library and defended it against any and all dangers that might present. He also made sure his inventory was correct at year's end.

Through the library's early years, readers of rare books were locked into wired alcoves for security, while studying the valuable titles. Three of these cages remain as they were on the opening of the library. Many of the collections in the library sit on the shelves allocated to them by Marsh and by Elias Bouhéreau, the first librarian. Marsh's own collection of books was bequeathed to the library by a successor. Other librarians that followed continued the collection of suitable titles for the library. The present library contains more than

25,000 books in its catalogue from to the sixteenth, seven-teenth and eighteenth centuries, relating to medicine, law, science, travel, navigation, mathematics, music, surveying and classical literature.

It is said that the ghost of Marsh wanders about the library seeking one particular note in one particular volume. The incident that caused him so much angst in his living days occurred a few years before the library opened. So, it would appear that the note his ghost is said to seek is in a book that was in his possession before the library that bears his name was built at all.

Marsh had been appointed Provost of Trinity on the nomination of James Butler, Duke of Ormonde, Chancellor and Lord Lieutenant, who was the *de facto* ruler of Ireland in the king's name. Marsh resigned as Provost when he was appointed Bishop of Ferns. Narcissus, while still Protestant Archbishop of Dublin, lived as a bachelor in the Palace of St Sepulchre beside the Cathedral. He arranged for his niece, Grace Marsh, to take care of housekeeping for him. Grace bore the same name as Narcissus' late mother. Grace was aged nineteen and wished to enjoy life as a young woman might best do in seventeenth-century Dublin Church and academic circles. She may have found her new surround-ings, lifestyle and the strict discipline of the archbishop's domain constricting and sought excitement from another gentleman of her acquaintance. For on 10 September 1695 Narcissus was discussing matters matrimonial with his diary. He wrote:

> This evening betwixt 8 and 9 of the clock at night my niece Grace Marsh (not having the fear of God before her eyes) stole privately out of my house at St. Sepulchre's and (as is reported) was that night married to Chas. Proby vicar of Castleknock in a Tavern and was bedded there with him - Lord consider my affliction.

She was, according to Narcissus, married to Charles before they were bedded, and he was, it appears, an ordained minister of some Protestant persuasion, else he could not have married at all. The fear of God might be read then as fear of the archbishop as representative of God, a fear which Grace seemed to have had none of at all. Or perhaps, she believed that if she had informed Narcissus of her plan to marry the vicar of Castleknock the archbishop might have demurred. A popular twist in the story is that Grace left a note for her Uncle Narcissus in a book in his home before she eloped, telling him of her proposed course of action. But the learned man did not find that note in time, and never did, or so it would appear from his subsequent peregrinations through his huge collection of books.

The archbishop was to live on for a further eighteen years during which the story took another turn. Grace returned to live with him in his declining years, with or without Chas the curate we cannot say. Narcissus Marsh died on 2 November 1713 in his seventy-fifth year. Once dead, Narcissus began to haunt his library. The ghost is said to frequent the inner gallery, which contains what was formerly his own private library. The spectre moves in and out among the bookcases, taking down books from the shelves, and occasionally throwing them down on the reader's desk as if in passion, anger or frustration. Nonetheless, ever the neat scholar, he is said to always leaves the library in perfect order, when he is through with

his throwing. Some librarians occupying the rooms below believed in the ghost upstairs, others did not. Although such disbelief is subjective, for when one fears an unexplained movement or noise from above, it is difficult to shrug each time and say that it was nothing.

Grace, the runaway teenager of the seventeenth century, lived to be eighty-five years old. Her remains are buried in the same tomb as her uncle the archbishop. Which begs the question: why does Grace not just tell him in which book lies the note of elopement? If in fact there ever was such a note. What would she have done had her powerful uncle found the note and held her in the house while he had a word with the vicar from Castleknock about his marriage prospects? Then again, perhaps the ghost who shuffles through the library is not Narcissus at all. Perhaps it is the ghost of the unknown Dubliner. Whoever it is, the library was formally incorporated in 1707 by an Act of Parliament, a transcript of which reads:

> An Act passed 1707 for settling and preserving a public library for ever in the house for that purpose built by His Grace Narcissus now Lord Archbishop of Armagh, on part of the Ground belonging to the Archbishop of Dublin's Palace, Near to the City of Dublin.

Amen to that.

27

FITS MAN

Bertie the baker lived on Dorset Street in the north of Dublin City. He was a generous person at heart and liked to help out his fellow man whenever he could. He was, however, a businessman first and foremost and he had to sell his bread and cakes at a profit. His customers knew this and graced him with their patronage. Bertie's Bakery, with its small shop front, was willed to him by his father who started the business when Bertie was but a baby.

The shop prospered. Even people that had moved away to other places would travel to Dorset Street on Saturdays to buy Bertie's brown bread to go with the weekend fry-ups. He found himself selling to the sons and daughters of the people that had bought from his father. But if he attracted the good customers, he also attracted the bad customers who moaned and complained about everything, in the hope that they would receive a discount or something for free. Usually Bertie made some little gesture to them when no one else was around. For he had learnt that such complainers were quite good customers if you thought about them in a different way. For them to have the right to make representations to him as the proprietor, they had to establish a relationship in the first place as paying customers. So, he would resist at first and then give in, saying that this was definitely the last time that this was going to happen. Apart from their never-ending quest for a discount, they were excellent customers.

None of which went unnoticed by Charley the local fool who hung around the shop for the smell of freshly baked bread and the sight of the cakes in the glass-fronted display shelves. To look at him, you would not think there was anything amiss. Charley was a neat and tidy man, but that small piece of the jigsaw puzzle that creates a functioning mind was mislaid. Bertie tolerated, more than welcomed, Charley's presence in the premises.

To remove Charley from the shop, Bertie occasionally asked him to do a small errand. Charley was always pleased to be asked. He always returned faster than Bertie would have thought possible or seemly. But since none of the people he sent bread or cakes to with Charley ever mentioned anything amiss, he continued to employ Charley in this way every now and again. This suited Charley, who was not a man that was in love with the concept of regular employment but who was pleased to serve as the baker's ambassador as needs be.

One Saturday afternoon, as Bertie was winding up sales for the weekend, he asked Charley to deliver a special cake of brown bread to a gentleman that lived across the river on Eustace Street in Temple Bar. Off Charley went with the street address memorised in his head and a lift to his step. He was careful that one foot did not trip up the other on the way. It was the last time that Bertie could rely on Charley as a messenger. For Charley was the victim of a minor street riot that erupted on O'Connell Street following a protest march for something or other. Stones were thrown at the police for so long and in such a sustained manner that a snatch squad ran into the crowd to arrest the ringleaders, during which Charley received a blow of a baton to the head which felled him where he stood.

Ever afterwards, Charley suffered from seizures which made him fall down and thrash about in a very disturbing manner. At least it was disturbing to onlookers, for Charley blanked out when it happened and was unperturbed by the experience, though he was always sore in places afterwards. Bertie was distressed by Charley's fits on a human level, but also, from a business point of view, he could hardly have a jiggling Charley rolling around the floor when he was taking an order for a birthday cake from a client who might not know Charley and the cause of the damage to the side of his brain. One day, Bertie asked Charley to stay inside while he closed the shop at the end of trading. He asked Charley to tell him what the doctors had said, whether there was any sign of a complete recovery and whether Charley had any advance notice of one of these seizures. The doctors were still working on it, Charley informed Bertie, but seeing a chance of enriching himself he said that sometimes he was able to know when an episode was likely to come along. There was a kind of a tingling in his head and a sense of having seen everything that was going to happen before. He wondered sometimes if he was a little psychic.

Did Bertie think he was psychic? Not with his record of backing losing horses with Bertie's money the baker almost replied, but he kept his counsel, for there is no wit in besting a slow mind. He came to an arrangement with Charley that if he felt he was going to have a seizure, he would tell Bertie and he would make sure that someone kept an eye on Charley and that medical aid arrived as soon as possible. A short time afterwards, Charley came into the shop and told Bertie he was going to collapse any moment now. True to his word, Bertie closed up shop and brought Charley to the hospital where doctors agreed that Charley should be in their care. Still and all, Charley was discharged not so long after that and life returned to normal in the bakery where the early-morning smell of fresh bread continued to lend its enticing aroma to the street. It was a while before Charley wandered in again with the same premonition. This time, he asked if he could empty his pockets into a tin beneath the counter for safekeeping while he was away. Bertie reluctantly agreed to this strange request. When Charley was gone to sit in the hospital's interminable accident and emergency queue, Bertie looked in the tin. All it contained was a small amount of money, a very old and small pen-knife and an unlikely picture of a glamorous woman who was most definitely not related to Charley. This then, was Charley's treasure.

Bertie was ashamed of himself for having breached the confidence of an afflicted man. He thought about this in the days that followed. Then, before Charley arrived back in to claim his goods, Bertie counted up the money in the tin. He made a quick calculation and added another third to the total from his own cash drawer. Charley collected his property but returned the following day in puzzlement. How had his money grown? Why was there more there than he had left? Bertie said he had put a little extra in as a bonus for all the good work Charley had done for the bakery and its clients. This pleased Charley and when next he went off to the hospital, he made a point of telling Bertie that he had placed his remaining cash in the tin and he would be back in a few days to collect it. When he collected it there was always that little bit extra there for him again. Charley was not that much of a fool that he could not count the windfall that appeared each time in his tin. Bertie noticed the frequency of Charley's seizure forecasts increased shortly after this. They stepped up until hardly a week went past without at least three warnings being given by the stricken Charley. Bertie also noticed that the amount on deposit increased each time which in due course also increased the sum total due on reclamation. After a while, it rose to the point where Bertie was contributing half a week's wages to Charley's recuperation fund.

If Charley was in fact suffering such a regular number of seizures then he would hardly have the strength to stand up, never mind time to recover between bouts. Matters deteriorated somewhat in the week when Charley declared the approach of an episode twice in the one day. The first was about 11 o'clock in the morning. Charley duly took himself off to the hospital where he was immediately discharged upon admittance. He came back, collected his tin and his little divvy, and left. He returned at three o'clock in the afternoon and repeated the exercise. Bertie considered cancelling the top-up, but since he had started it of his own free will, he did not like to do so. He considered removing some of the capital in the first place so the end calculation would be different, but thought better of that in turn.

It was while he was contemplating such matters that his mind was made up for him by two callers. The first man asked to buy some brown bread. Bertie had bagged it for him when the man said he thought he felt faint and was like to fall down in a seizure. While Bertie said nothing the man asked the baker if he would go through his pockets before the ambulance arrived and remove the money he had in his pocket. All Bertie had to do was mind it for the patient until he returned in a day or two. Bertie refused and the man slammed out the door, setting the bell above it jangling with crossness. Next, a middle-aged woman called in that afternoon to enquire if Bertie was the kind-hearted baker that kept care of valuables for people while they were inside and gave them money when they came back. It was after she was sent packing that Charley arrived in to say he was not feeling at all well and could he leave his few bob in the tin as usual. Bertie said of course he could but he wanted to put matters on a sensible and fair footing between them. Charley was not sure what that meant but he agreed anyway. Bertie said he wanted to give Charley a little more dough than he had been able to do in the recent past. Charley agreed.

Imagine Charley's surprise then when he arrived back into the shop and Bertie presented him with the tin, sealed and wrapped in splendid Christmas paper though it was mid-summer and not mid-winter. Bertie made Charley promise to take the tin home with him and not to open it until he was alone. A very excited Charley hurried home and tore off the wrapping paper to reveal his familiar tin box. His fingers could hardly prise the lid open quickly enough. The tin felt deliciously heavy. There must be lots in it. Inside, he found all the money he had placed in there, he found his pen-knife and the picture of a forgotten film star and he found a small fruit scone. He searched in vain for Bertie's bonus money but there was none. The only dough he had received was this scone, which when he squeezed was approaching staleness. He set it aside in disappointment.

It only goes to show that you can try the patience of even the most patient baker once too often. And that when it comes to getting rid of chancers and hangers-on, you cannot beat a nice stale fruit scone, freshly baked a week ago when everyone was a lot younger and had a lot more sense.

28

HOLY COAL

In Dublin, halfway through the last century, people were so poor that they didn't even know they were poor. For if you never had anything, you never feel the want of it. There was no central heating; you just retired for the night with the overcoat thrown over you in the bed. It was the same coat you wore during the day. You tried to keep the big buttons from taking your eye out if you had a nightmare. The pockets were generally emptied to show the difference between the waking and the sleeping state. An empty coat was fine for a blanket substitute whereas bulging pockets were not quite safe, for who knew what might be squashed in the turmoil of the night. Many is the man afflicted by demons that went to bed hale and hearty and woke up the following morning with a pair of black eyes after a poor night's sleep. Few people noticed, however, for most were buried in their own heavy coats in an attempt to keep the chill from their bones until the warm days returned.

A domestic fire doubled as a cooking fire when pots or kettles were warmed by the rising heat from the burning coals. Not everyone could afford real coal, however. Many was the house that got by without internal wooden doors at all, as they had been taken down and used for firewood. The local coalman did the best he could to find inexpensive coal that would burn for his customers. The problem was that cheap coal produced more smoke than heat and so a balance had to be struck between economy and utility. So he was happy when his buying skills on behalf of his customers was recognised by charity groups who contracted him to deliver free winter fuel to their clients on their behalf. Since these were local residents, Jemmy the coalman knew them all.

These included two unmarried sisters, who lived in one room in a tenement with a window so small that a mouse would be hard set to see out of it. There was very little light in the room. It had a fireplace with a small range, where they cooked whatever they had to eat. They always had sufficient food for their needs, given that they were highly skilled in accessing whatever relief was available to the needy. A table, two chairs and a pair of single beds against opposite walls was the rest of it. In the corner, at the foot of Betty the eldest's bed, was a tea chest to hold whatever fuel they had to burn on the day, be it coal, a bit of a door, a few logs dropped in by a neighbour, or just coiled up day-old newspaper obtained from Frank the newsagent on the corner.

They qualified for charitable assistance since Molly, the youngest, with the coiled long hair, had taken to the bed, with ten Woodbines a day, years before. She was not in the habit of getting out of it overmuch and especially not if the local priest or anyone associated with charitable causes was about to see her. She stayed in the nest on this cold winter's morning when white frost glistened on everything, hair crackled in the cold and those that had jobs to go to slid down the road to work. Those with bicycles tried to walk beside them with some dignity until they came to a dry patch that they could try cycling along.

Deliveries were made on old wheezing lorries that were often reluctant to start in the morning, especially if there had been freezing temperatures the night before. Jemmy's coal lorry wanted to take the day off, on this day, but Jemmy needed to be about his work. He especially needed to deliver fuel to the list of charity clients so he could present a bill for goods supplied.

An awkward class of a man called Fitzer lived nearby, who had set his mind on becoming the coalman's apprentice and who hung about in case he would be hired by the coalman. Fitzer thought it would be a fine thing to sit high up in the coal lorry and wave at people as they passed by on the streets of the town. When asked by Jemmy, Fitzer agreed to give the lorry a push to start it rolling down an adjacent hill on this freezing cold morning. A few more people passing by put their shoulder to the tail end of the malachite green lorry and away she went down the gradient, without the benefit of any combustive power at all. She was powered by gravity alone and steered by a calm Jemmy in a straight line, to get the benefit of the fall of the ground on the way to the lower street below.

Jemmy gently dropped the hurtling lorry into gear half-way down. She started up with a shudder and a great cloud of smoke. The swirling smoke covered Mrs Burke's cat who, quite coincidentally, had been run over and killed by the lorry in the excitement of the morning. The cat was called Larry after her late husband. It had been sleeping on the chassis of the lorry as close as it could get to the warmth of the cooling engine through the cold night. Larry, the man that is, had brought home a cat long ago and after the original Larry the cat died, and the cat that replaced that one died, all of its replacements were named Larry in honour of the first cat who was sorely missed by Mrs Burke.

Given that the morning had long since started and that he was now late, Jemmy made the further error of hiring Fitzer for the day to deliver the coal with him. The first stop was at the tenement where the two sisters resided. By then, Mrs Burke was caterwauling over the body of the defunct Larry. She asked Jeremiah, the town fool, if he would fetch a priest to say a prayer for the dead cat, it being one of God's creatures. She reasoned that nobody could prove if a man had a soul or not and therefore, equally, you could not say that a cat did not have a soul to be prayed for.

Jeremiah duly called to the priest's house and told the man of the cloth, who was new to the area, that Larry Burke had been run over and requested that he go and say a few prayers. The priest, whose own car would not start as a result of the heavy frost, hurried off determinedly down the road, wishing to please his new flock. It would make a good impression on a new community, if he arrived promptly when called.

By then, Fitzer had managed to mis-hear Jemmy's precise instructions on delivering coal to the sisters' first-floor back flat where they awaited their ten stone of free coal, enough for a frugal week's burning. Fitzer was to turn right when he went in the door of the sisters' room. He was to empty the open bag of black tumbling coal in the wooden tea chest before him. He would know in the dark where this was by bumping his knees gently against the plywood side of the box. These were the careful instructions given by the master coalman to the apprentice.

Fitzer turned left, not right; he walked until he met resistance on his legs, as instructed; he then emptied the bag of coal down on top of Molly, who was sleeping in her bed and certainly not anticipating a pummelling on high delivered by a strange man. She rose up with a strangled cry and a selection of curses that would take the scales off a silver salmon freshly poached from the river. In her fist was a fine shaped lump of black coal. Her other fist held the same. Knowing instantly what he had done wrong, Fitzer took off for his life towards the daylight at the other end of the long hall. He was followed by flying lumps of coal as Molly rose to her full wrath. A lust for vengeance overtook her; the kind that could only consume a somnolent woman roused to painful wakefulness by a flying idiot.

Fitzer reached the street just as the perspiring priest was passing by on his way to bless a dead cat. He was soon confronted by a dancing Molly who, he had been told, had been bedridden for the past ten years, a hopeless case. Molly stopped dead realising the awful truth that was now revealed. She could walk. She could also curse, swear, run, and throw coal after a fleeing coalman's apprentice. A silence crept though the frozen street as Molly tried to smile. Jemmy came around from the back of the lorry where he had taken shelter. The priest wondered how long a dead soul generally waits around for the Last Rites to be performed over it.

It was then that the inspired voice of Betty floated down from the tenement steps above. 'Glory be to God', she cried. 'That coal is blessed. It's made my poor unfortunate sister rise up and walk again. Glory be to God. And the coalman.' she added, just in case, for Jemmy could be contrary at times and might delay next week's delivery if sufficiently vexed.

Fitzer the apprentice kept going and went to stay with his sister in Mullingar for a fortnight, for safety. The priest, when he heard he was hurrying to bless a dead cat, stayed and prayed with Molly and Betty instead for the miracle of the Holy Coal even if he knew in his heart and soul that something was dreadfully amiss in their collective minds. Jemmy drove off in the certain knowledge that the sisters were going to become faith healers for hire, the priest was going to go insanely mad at some stage, and Mrs Burke was going to be looking for a new cat from him. There was one thing he was sure of. He had seen a lot of things in his time, but he had never ever seen flying coal pass down the street before or since. It's the sort of thing you don't see much of at all in these days of prosperity in the new Ireland. More's the pity.

29

LUGS BRANNIGAN

Some people live their lives in as quiet and orderly a manner as possible, while others seem to want to cause as much disruption as they can. To deal with the disruption, a special unit of the police was drawn together in 1950s Dublin and lasted until the retirement of Detective Sergeant Lugs Brannigan, the man who was to lead it for so many years. His name struck fear into the hearts of criminals and disturbers of the peace alike. The shout that Lugs was on his way was often enough to scatter a crowd to their homes or lodging houses. They would immediately flee lest they be caught by the no-nonsense Brannigan and his men.

A Dubliner himself, born at the South Dublin Union on St James's Street, Jim Brannigan joined the Garda Síochána and doled out street justice in his own way though the 1930s and '40s. Such was the success of his rough and ready methods, that he was given a squad of like-minded officers to assist him in his work. Lugs Brannigan, or James Christopher Brannigan, or Jim Brannigan, was born on Little Christmas Day, 6 January 1910 and lived in his native city until his passing on 22 May 1986. He finished training as a garda in June 1931 in the Garda training depot in Phoenix Park, not far across the river from where he was born.

When street gangs presented a real problem to Dubliners and to their enjoyment of life in the capital, a robust response was called for, or so went official thinking. Lugs and his newly-formed crew were nicknamed the Brano Five Team. They formed a roving unit, from 1964 onwards, that was called out to trouble spots in Dublin, when ordinary beat policing was not succeeding. They used one car and one Bedford van as unit transport. The van carried two burly men and a number of Alsatian police dogs for crowd control. The car carried three more large police officers armed with regulation-issue batons and their fists and booted feet. This unit became well known around the dance halls and cinemas of Dublin, where young people met and where trouble could break out if one or other of the gangs had a mind to cause it. Late-night buses into problem areas of the city were followed by the unit anticipating disorder. A non-fare payer might have second thoughts on causing disruption when Brannigan boarded the bus to assist the bus conductor with his troublesome passenger. If the passenger was lucky, he was allowed to pay the fare and to sit down, if not, he was removed from the bus to face Lugs' justice.

The unit often patrolled the streets to keep order. Indeed, the claim is made that Brannigan sat through *Rock around the Clock* some ninety times, in his role as pacifier, when local Teddy Boys imitated international reaction and rioted throughout the showing of the film. On one occasion, an erring motorist on O'Connell Street managed to collide with the rear of the unit's van, as the van slowed to allow a garda speak to a group of loitering youths outside the cinema. Such was the power of Brannigan's name that the driver fell to uncontrollable shaking at the prospect of a meeting with Lugs Brannigan over minor damage to the van. Brannigan left another guard to take the details. A crowd soon gathered, giving Brannigan and his men the opportunity to show they were fair observers of the law in their own right.

While Brannigan was determined to put an end to street fighting in the city, he was an enthusiastic boxer himself. During the 1930s, he was a member of the Garda Boxing

Club, fighting at cruiser-weight, light-heavyweight and heavyweight and eventually winning the Leinster heavy-weight title in 1937. While his fists were considered as potential lethal weapons, he often offered a prisoner the choice of fighting him one-to-one and going free, or being charged in court with an offense. Such was the weight that Brannigan carried with the judiciary, a case brought by him was reasonably sure of success.

The unit was successful in pacifying smaller gangs and hard men alike. Brannigan's biggest difficulty was with the Animal Gang, whose numbers in any street fight could range as high as 100. They were bent on fighting with pota-toes studded with razor blades, batons, knives, bottles and anything else that could cause injury to an opponent. Garda reports of the mid-1930s show the feuding Animal Gang marauded through Dublin, engaging in fierce pitched bat-tles on the streets, to the terror of all in their way. Members of the gang gatecrashed dancehalls, where they attacked people against whom they carried grudges. Garda reports said that the Animal Gang had no political motivation and that unlike the European phenomenon of fascist gangs spreading terror through the continent's cities, the Animal Gang were simply hooligans.

It is said, that on one night, when Lugs Brannigan caught up with a number of gang members in a dance hall, the assembled patrons parted like the Red Sea before Moses, as he took the three hooligans outside and there dispensed his own judgement and punishment on them. Brannigan's crusade against the Animal Gang came to a head at Baldoyle Racecourse in north County Dublin in 1940. He and other gardaí arrested seven prominent members of the gang at the course. Four more were taken into custody later that night. All eleven were sentenced to prison terms in Mountjoy and the gang was dealt a fatal blow.

Things were not easy for ordinary people in Dublin in the 1950s, when unemployment and emigration were the norm for many. Idle hands make work for the devil they used to say, and it was no surprise to Lugs Brannigan that as many as ten gangs formed in the city. Nightly battles and scuffles broke out as they fought for control of territory. In the middle of the mayhem Brannigan was to be found trying to stem the spread of gang warfare. It was Brannigan's unofficial warfare that courts often turned a blind eye to when complaints of garda misbehaviour were made by defence counsel to judges. Especially when it came to a Brannigan charge, since it was well known that Lugs gave the culprit a chance to fight it out or come to court. Judges were not about to allow a defendant to walk away without just cause.

Some lawbreakers, on hearing that Lugs Brannigan was looking for them, simply took the boat across to Britain, for a while or for good, to escape a certain beating or a jail term. Such a course of action served Brannigan's desire for a quiet city just the same.

Brannigan was a boxer and a boxing referee of such toughness that he continued to be a referee for amateur boxers well into his seventies and past retirement. Nonetheless, fighting members of street gangs had its effect on the bodies of the gardaí that faced the hooligan element in late-night Dublin City. Many of the fighters were armed with knives, the weapon of choice for street fighting. Many would throw razor spuds at their opponents or try to get in close to tear the skin off the face of their opponent with the exposed blades. Many were simply drunk and ugly and would attack from any direction without warning, with any weapon they could find. Many just sank their teeth into their foe's body. Others left welt marks on flesh where they struck with studded leather belts. Many people sported multi-coloured bruises for months afterwards. Knuckledusters were worn on the hand and their metal teeth tore skin away from flesh and left scars that took a long time to heal. Scars would remain on both lawmaker and lawbreaker.

Brannigan suffered many attacks over the years. By the time he finished with his life in the Garda, his body was like a relief road map of the city, with souvenirs of the many confrontations he endured with some of the most violent and crazed people in Dublin. He was philosophical about the injuries his own physique endured, saying that he gave as good as he got. Far from being self conscious of his scars, Brannigan was happy enough to discuss his physical souvenirs with anyone who had a serious interest in them. For display purposes, the remnants of the punishment inflicted on his legs by all and sundry were a source of particular fascination. The boot was put into him with cheap boots, shoes, runners, bare feet, steel toe-capped working boots and more in his time. All of which left his legs crossed with a mass of scar tissue from his wounds. There were lumps on his legs where there should not have been lumps, and hollows where the flesh had caved in from some attack and had never returned to normal. Still, it did not stop him refereeing amateur boxing matches in his retirement for many years.

A particular story was told of a city prostitute who reported to him that a false client had stolen her money and would not return it to her. Lugs is said to have followed the man to where he was celebrating his new-found wealth and retrieved the woman's earnings for her. One can imagine how surprised and shocked the man was to discover that Lugs Brannigan wanted a word with him in the street outside the hotel.

Jim Brannigan left the Garda as a detective sergeant in 1973, after more than forty years' service. He retired to the quietness of Summerhill in County Meath where his interest turned to raising budgerigars. He worked part-time as a personal bodyguard for visiting celebrities and occasionally as a doorman at city centre late-night venues. Lugs Brannigan passed away in 1986, by which time policing methods had changed and society no longer had any desire for the rough and ready justice that was the hallmark of Lugs Brannigan, boxer, pacifier, garda and Dubliner.

30

CHRISTMAS COOKING

Many people on the run during the War of Independence took refuge in a family home at Christmas in Dublin. While it was a dangerous thing to do, some people accepted the risk for the sake of the season. Once St Stephen's Day had been and gone it was back to days of danger, filled with the fear of what might happen next.

When hostilities ended, many of the fighters simply took their weapons home with them rather than hand them in. They hid their arms away, just as the rebels of yore would conceal pikes in the thatch for future use. This practice left it wide open during subsequent arguments of any side to claim that if matters went much further, the gun would have to be sent for to settle the argument. It rarely was sent for, but the thought was there just the same.

A chance remark was made in one particular house leading to the belief that the gun on the high nail in the kitchen of the house was a real gun, and what's more, was loaded for action. Of course it wasn't a genuine gun at all. It was an old-fashioned toy gun made of some metal that was both heavy and rough. It was a cap gun that detonated a single cap at a time, thrilling children of times past. For them, it sounded just the same as Napoleon's artillery might have sounded in battle, had they been there. Imagination is a powerful thing. It had been the plaything of the eldest boy of the family but when he discovered girls he had no further use for toy guns. His sights were on other targets, forevermore.

His father, the postmaster and an old rebel, painted it gun-metal black and when it was dry he added another coat to make it look really dark. Then, he climbed onto a high chair and drove a nail into the wall of the high-ceilinged kitchen where he hung the gun by its trigger guard, above the fireplace. It was the most effective security device imaginable, for it seemed to anyone with a mind set for mischief that it was a real weapon and what was more it was near at hand to a man that knew how to use it.

It stayed where it was, until one Christmas Eve, when some layabouts thought it a good idea to rob the post office of its Christmas funds, despite the deterrent hanging upon the nail in the kitchen. By then, Pauric the postmaster had finished work for the day and all the Christmas payments had been given out and all the savings accounts had been raided by people withdrawing funds to buy last minute presents. In short, when the three local robbers launched their daring raid, there was as little money in the post office as ever there would be.

The streets had grown quiet as people wound down their activities in expectation of a family reunion around the Christmas tree. The darkened premises were locked and barred from the front. So the route for the robbers was around the back and through the household quarters. That way took them through the kitchen where the Christmas cake was sitting and where a Christmas pudding, wrapped in its cocoon of greased cloth, was hanging from a cross door. Pauric's wife May, who was the power behind the post office throne, was not there. She had gone to the city to buy her family's treats, presents and surprises for the great day. The three robbers, Petey, Liam and Maurice, easily gained access to the kitchen and from there to the post office itself. They were bitterly disappointed to discover the cash they were expecting to load up in their bags had flown the coop. Gone!

To make sure that any mad robbers did no damage to the till or the safe, Pauric had left both open wide. That way, he would not have to pay for repairs when they attacked them only to find there was no reward for their efforts to be had. While Petey and Liam wandered about the empty post office in the hope of finding a pot of gold, Maurice found his way into the kitchen where he sat at the big kitchen table to have a think beside the glowing range. The heat was nice; the range gave off a comfortable warmth. An intoxicating smell of Christmas baking, completed that very afternoon, wafted around Maurice's disappointed head. As he came to terms with his disappointment, he found himself softly humming an almost-forgotten Christmas carol to himself.

At this point the others arrived in the kitchen on the hunt for something they could take with them. If they could not find cash, they would settle for anything they could steal and turn into ready money. They were pleasantly surprised to discover several unopened bottles of Christmas cheer in a press in a corner. No sooner had they come upon this treasure, than they began to cheer themselves up with copious glasses of amber liquid. They were soon on a roll and the first bottle was emptied quickly. Since a bird never flew on one wing, they opened another bottle, and then another for luck. Then, Petey who was afflicted all his life with a sweet tooth declared they should have a slice of homemade Christmas cake to go with the sup.

As it happened, the absent May was known across four parishes for the quality of her Christmas cakes and puddings. She had a nice sideline in providing the same to a select clientele. Her baking was so popular that to get onto her list, you had to wait until someone died. So, when Petey took a large carving knife and chopped out chunks from the Christmas cake that was reserved for May's own table, he had inadvertently crossed the Rubicon. Petey made sure his two companions had the same size wedge of iced Christmas cake as he did. So, it was natural, that with a lump of cake each to consume and drink to go with it, the three buddies would stay longer than normal at the scene of a crime. It was also a given that they would grow drowsy with warmth both inside and out.

Liam was the first to nod off. His heavy head lolled on his breast; his mouth lay open and a trickle of sweet saliva eventually fell from his mouth to his chest. The others toned down their singing out of respect for a tired and discouraged colleague. That was the way the house lay when May came into the kitchen with her full shopping bags bouncing against her tired legs. Another person arriving into their home to find three layabouts dozing before the fire would have made a fuss, might even have run away to safety, might have called for the gardaì, but May was cut from different cloth. She was the wife of a retired rebel and she decided to renew the armed struggle against the invaders. May had seen off more than a few mad robbers when an ill-considered raid was made on the front of house. Now they were in her kitchen.

She stood for a moment, in the middle of the floor, with her bags resting against her ankles. It was cold outside and she still had her heavy maroon top-coat buttoned up. She opened it a button at a time and took it off her before proceeding. May hauled a heavy wooden chair over to the side wall, as quietly as she could. She climbed up on the chair, balanced, and took the black gun down from its rusted nail, blowing the dust from it as she stepped back down again. Without disturbing the three sleeping cherubs, she removed a large saucepan from the press along with a number of lids of varying sizes. May stuck the gun in her belt and banged the saucepan and the lid together as hard as she could while shouting, 'Wake up, wake up, she has a gun.'

Petey leaped up first and stared down the barrel of the gun that May was now waving at them. Maurice joined him in his terror and it was not long before Liam was quaking in his boots beside them. All three were instantly contrite and if not exactly shocked into sobriety, they had at least stopped drooling into the glowing fire.

May gestured towards the door with the gun. Petey, who was by now awake the longest, took the first tentative step to safety. An irate housewife was likely to do anything with a gun, even if it was by accident, he reasoned. Being shot on purpose or by accident was all the same; you were still wounded or dead as luck would have it.

He stepped away, a step at a time. When the others saw that he was still alive they also stepped along. They held onto one another until they resembled a shuffling jelly with six feet and three heads, each more terrified than the other. Once at the open doorway they paused. On one side was a very cross woman with a gun, and on the other was black darkness outside where it might be safe to make a run for it. The jelly split open and they ran out of the house bumping and banging into one another when May shouted, 'Run, run, she has a gun. She's going to fire it.'

From that day onwards, not a man of them could tell whether they were followed by shots or if the noises they heard in the cold night air was the sound of saucepan lids hitting the door behind them. What was certain was that there was never another attempt to break into that business or that home. For word went about the town that May was a crack shot with the loaded pistol that hung on the rusty nail in the kitchen and nobody was prepared to argue with an Irish mother with a gun. It would be an argument nobody would ever win. For a loaded mother is a sight to behold.

31

THE HELLFIRE CLUB

Most Christian cities had a religious statue placed on a high point above the city as a symbol of piety to the faithful, and as a warning to evil to stay away from the protected people below. Dublin, for its part, had a long building perched atop the Dublin Mountains to the south of the city that was associated with the devil and devil worship. Not that the devil was said to be protecting his own in the town below, more like a few people had risen up to worship the devil as an alternative belief system, after being barred from their usual drinking haunt near Christ Church Cathedral. They went up the top of the mountain at Killakee, above Rathfarnham, and they indulged in all sorts of shenanigans, that were reportedly of so debased a character that any mortal soul that wandered in was left dumbstruck from then on from the experience. The mountain is more of a hill really at something around 390 metres, but the hills are referred to by Dubliners as the Dublin mountains. These are the things Dubliners believe. The hills are mountains. Fair enough. Someone in the past decided that and no one will now disagree. While the shooting lodge was not built quite at the crest of the hill, it still commanded a view over Dublin City, from Rathfarnham and Tallaght below it, right across to Phoenix Park to the west and Ireland's Eye and Howth Head on the far side of Dublin Bay to the north.

William Connolly who was Speaker of the Irish House of Commons had the house built on Mount Pelier Hill in 1725. Speaker Connolly as he was known, was one of the richest men in Ireland in his day. He built the club as a hunting lodge. All windows face north, perhaps for the view, perhaps for some other reason. A relic of a pre-historic passage tomb stood beside the site of the house. It was described as being made of large flat stones set edgewise. Inside were smaller stones collected into a heap. In the centre was a monolith nine feet high, six feet wide, and three feet thick. A similar stone about five or six feet high stood about sixty yards away. The cairn was destroyed without too much concern and the boulders were used in construction of the lodge. A slate roof was placed on top of the building, but was blown off in a great storm, shortly afterwards. Locals attributed this misfortune to bad luck accruing from the destruction of the cairn. In response Speaker Connolly built a massive arched roof of stones keyed together for greater interlocking strength, similar to what is seen in construction of an old stone bridge. This roof was so tough that it withstood the onslaught of wind or bad-luck from that day on. The flat stones from the ruined cairn were set edgewise in the roof and gaps were filled with gravel and mortar until a uniform surface was built up. Otherwise, the house was constructed of very rough and irregular materials, ill calculated to remain long in good repair, according to reports, which may offer a different explanation for why the roof took off in a mountain storm. Shoddy workmanship rarely stands before the forces of nature.

None of which did anything to quieten the unease of people in the neighbourhood who said no luck would ever return to the building or its users. After Connolly's death in 1729, the lodge lay empty and unused for some years until it was acquired by Richard Parsons and the Hellfire Club, from which it took its name for ever more. At this point the lodge attracted the interest of a number of Dublin rakes: moneyed and privileged layabouts.

The Hellfire clubs was started in England by Sir Francis Dashwood in Buckinghamshire. The club and its copy-cats became notorious for rumoured sexual orgies and occult activities. Richard Parsons, Earl of Rosse, established the Dublin Hellfire Club in 1735 where it became associated with excessive drinking of whiskey and bacchanalian pastimes. Club founder Parsons answered to the title of 'The King of Hell', what else. He is said to have dressed like Satan might very well do, with horns, wings and cloven hooves as part of his get-up. A chair was ritually left unoccupied for the devil or his emissary to sit upon. The first toast was always drunk in honour of the absent devil, who might join the assembly at any moment.

Perhaps it was the devil who masqueraded as a visitor to the house one dark night in Connolly's time. The stranger asked for lodging for the night. As was the custom he was granted overnight lodgings and treated hospitably. A card game was suggested. Everything was going well until one of the players let a card fall to the floor. Bending down to pick it up, he was shocked at what he saw beneath the well-cut leggings of the house guest. Leaning back up, he cried that the visitor had a cloven hoof in place of a foot. Once challenged, the story goes, Satan conjured up a clap of thunder and smoke which, when it cleared, left a reek of brimstone behind it. And a vanished guest.

The devil must have formed an attachment to the house for he was reputed to be a regular presence once the orgies of the Hellfire Club got going. However, Weston St John Joyce, in his 1912 *The Neighbourhood of Dublin*, wrote that while the Hellfire Club may have held some of its meetings in this house, it was tolerably certain that it was never one of the regular meeting places of that mysterious and iniquitous body, the ordinary rendezvous of which was the Eagle Tavern, on Cork Hill, beside Dublin Castle and just down the road from the Irish Commons on College Green. Someone else suggested that the boozers were asked not to patronise the Eagle Tavern any more and thus repaired to the top of the Dublin mountains to continue their hedonistic interests, or to skull a few more drinks in private, depending on who you believe.

The hunting lodge included two large rooms and a hall on the upper floor. A small loft sat over the parlour and entrance hall. The hall door was reached by a flight of steps. On the ground level was a large kitchen, servants' quarters and a number of small rooms.

Scalteen was said to be their favourite drink. It was made from half a pint of whiskey, half a pound of butter and six eggs. It was taken red-hot for best result. It was said that scalteen would make a corpse walk as it was so powerful it would put the life back into anyone, man or beast, dead or alive. It was a great reviver to those who came in off a winter hill, with the cold wrapped around them like a mountain mist around a lone bush. The advice was that once it was swallowed by the drinker, he should go to bed while he was still able to do so. Such a powerful intoxicant swallowed freely and frequently could explain some of the reports of the devil himself appearing in the Hellfire Club.

Many are the stories of strong men seeing Nick himself smiling at them from the bottom of a bottle of strong spirits, never mind the addition of intoxicating eggs and butter to the mix. Given that most of those present in the building on these occasions were intoxicated in some way or another, either through over-imbibing in scalteen or by hereditary in-breeding causing delusions of the mind what credence can be put to the tale of a cleric who found himself on the grounds one dark night?

A large black cat was the centre of the devil-worshippers attention, noted the clergyman. The cleric was soon hauled into the circle by some of the devil's men. But the cleric shook himself free from his mortal captors to turn

his attention to the hissing feline. He prayed and called for the demon to be cast out by a power far greater than his own. Whatever happened, it is said, the unfortunate cat was torn asunder and a demon appeared, striking fear into all present. Once more, having had the required effect of terrifying the living daylights out of everyone, the devil took himself off about his business. He left, this time through the roof, smashing down the ceiling as he went, causing even more discomfort to the assembled onlookers.

Whatever was going on inside the building when the club was in session was enough to frighten the daylights out of any civilian that happened to become embroiled in it. A young local farmer was intrigued by the tales of debauchery and wild drinking. He, it seems, thought it a good idea to ramble along that way so that he might see for himself what was going on. So, he climbed up the hill by himself, one evening, when it was just about time for the shenanigans to begin. One supposes he was a free spirit and like most young men of farming stock, not unaware of the mating rituals of many species of animal both on and off the farm. So he would be able to take a broad view of whatever he witnessed. He may have thought he might just take a peek in through the windows on his first visit, but some members of the club are said to have grabbed him and brought him inside to meet their fellow devil worshippers.

People who knew him said he was found the following morning, wandering around the area in a state of post traumatic shock. The young farmer was unable to speak and he never regained his hearing or speaking senses after that.

Dublin's Hellfire Club lasted only as long as 'The King of Hell' was around; it fell apart following the death of the libertine Parsons in 1741 at thirty-nine years of age. The building burnt down during some bacchanal ritual or another and became a ruin on the top of a hill overlooking Dublin, though it lives on in Dublin folklore. From time to time, there are reports of satanic rituals being re-enacted there. In the absence of the devil himself they are likely to be exciting only to the participants for as long as they remain at the site of the Dublin Hellfire Club.

For the devil is well known to be a liar and a yarnspinner to gullible souls. Still, he has his work cut out for him when Dubliners start to tell stories for everyone has a story to tell if the listener will just draw nigh and hark to a tale well told.